)03

A COMMAND
OF THE HEART

A COMMAND
OF THE HEART

•

J. P. MATHEWS

AVALON BOOKS
THOMAS BOUREGY AND COMPANY, INC.
401 LAFAYETTE STREET
NEW YORK, NEW YORK 10003

There is no ship named USS *Lockwood* (FFG-540) on the
active Navy List, although a frigate of this name (DE-1064)
previously served in the Fleet. The characters, similarly, are
fictitious, and any resemblance to actual persons, living or
deceased, is purely coincidental. Navy, Coast Guard and Joint
commands are represented fictionally, not necessarily as they
operate in real life. Insofar as this book addresses military
policies, tactical operations and doctrine, they are those of the
author alone. They do not represent official views of the
Department of the Navy, the U.S. Coast Guard, the Department
of Defense, or the Department of Transportation.

PRINTED IN THE UNITED STATES OF AMERICA
ON ACID-FREE PAPER
BY HADDON CRAFTSMEN, SCRANTON, PENNSYLVANIA

This book is dedicated to the officers, men, and women of the United States Navy and Coast Guard, who go down to the sea in ships in the service of their country.

They have built the reputation of the United States on the oceans of the world as a nation that sends its ships where the freedom and safety of others, and the welfare of America's friends and our national interest, are threatened.

America is greater for their efforts, safer for their dedication, more assured of its freedom for their sacrifice.

Grateful acknowledgment is extended to:

Linda Dunlap, RN, an accomplished and talented author who reminded me gently that writing about sailors and writing about women who are sailors are two different things.

Dean Warren, whose sharp analytic eye found many changes that enhanced the manuscript.

The Western Hemisphere Group, U.S. Atlantic Fleet, Mayport, Florida, and Captain Jim Hanna for advice on Caribbean operations and the tactical maneuvering of the U.S. Navy's FFG-7 class guided missile frigates.

The Office of Information, Navy Department, for information, photographs and data that helped ensure the technical accuracy of the book.

Commander Chris Panos, USN (Ret.), a naval aviator and P-3 pilot, for his advice on that aspect of antisubmarine warfare.

—J.P.M.

Winter Springs, Florida
May 1996

Chapter One

"Right full rudder, come to course one eight zero." Lieutenant (junior grade) Kathleen Ann Shannon's crisp order rang through the pilothouse of the guided missile frigate USS *Lockwood* in the western North Atlantic. Her glossy black hair rested in a tight bun above the collar of a khaki uniform shirt. Blue eyes peered through binoculars focused on the horizon as she stood on the bridge wing a few feet away.

Ahead through light haze, the tanker *Merrimack* lumbered along, waiting to take *Lockwood* alongside. As Officer of the Deck, the slender twenty-four-year-old woman maneuvered the sleek 4,000-ton warship, and held in her hands the lives of its two hundred men and eight women.

Seaman Mark Wellinger, the helmsman, sat with his hand on the ship's four-inch brass wheel. He hesitated for an instant, and glanced toward the male junior officer of the deck.

"*Now*, Seaman Wellinger!" Kathy barked, the glasses still at her eyes. She heard the wheel snap quickly to the right. The ship heeled, bent gracefully into the whitecapped

1

sea, turning into the wind. Biting Wellinger for his delay made the point, she thought.

"All ahead two-thirds," she ordered.

"All ahead two-thirds, aye, ma'am," the sailor at the engine order telegraph cried out immediately, and pushed forward what looked like a car's floor-mounted gearshift handle. The ship's controls were miniature, she thought, compared with the older ones. The console that controlled them looked more like that of an aircraft than a warship.

"Steady on course one eight zero, ma'am," Wellinger shouted.

"Very well," she acknowledged. "Steady as you go."

Kathy walked in, and reached for the sound-powered phone behind the helmsman. "Captain, Bridge. Tanker bears one seven eight, range seven miles. Request permission to set the fueling detail."

"Make it so," the commanding officer's voice answered over the phone.

She turned to the boatswain's mate of the watch. "Boats, set the fueling detail, port side, please."

The tall man nodded and stepped to the ship's announcing system. The sharp, traditional shriek of his pipe preceded the order passed throughout the ship.

Within a minute, she saw men and women hurry to fueling connections on the upper deck called the 03 level. This mixed-manning demonstration was a first in small combatants. How well the Navy thought the female sailors did their jobs would determine the future of women in small combatant ships like frigates and destroyers, she thought.

The frigate's captain, Commander John Taylor, in his late thirties with gray streaks in his dark hair, climbed up the ladder behind the bridge and slid quietly into the leather-covered chair on the starboard side of the pilot house.

Kathy felt herself become tense as *Lockwood* surged forward toward closure with the tanker. A minor steering error by the helmsman, or a few seconds of her own inattention, could provoke a deadly collision. Although she'd done refuelings before, the responsibility always ran her adrenaline. Minutes later, she guided the streamlined missile ship silently into place alongside the hulking tanker, as both ships plowed through waters two hundred miles from the Florida coast.

An amateur ship's band of a half dozen tanker crewmen belted out the strains of "Hold That Tiger," in surprisingly good Dixieland style. Foaming ocean coursed through the eighty-foot gap between the ships with the speed of an approach to Niagara. *Lockwood*'s bow pitched up and down as waves washed her sides.

Linehandling guns on the tanker fired nylon filaments across the water between the ships onto the frigate's upper deck. Heavier ropes followed, until *Lockwood* crewmen finally hauled the massive fuel hoses aboard and connected them into two fueling connections which led to the ship's tanks decks below.

To Kathy, Commander Taylor concealed anxiety as he watched every move from his bridge chair, rubbing the unlit pipe in his hand. As Boats had said while passing the word, "The smoking lamp is out throughout the ship while taking on fuel." The skipper would rather do this fueling drill himself. She knew, however, that he must train his younger officers in the elaborate ballet learned and perfected only by practice.

Five-foot-two Quartermaster Third Class Susan Thomas had relieved Wellinger at the helm when the fueling detail was set. Her brown eyes moved with fixed concentration between the ship's heading and the gyrocompass repeater nearby. Thomas guided the 450-foot-long frigate within a half-degree of course, making both ships appear motionless as they steamed parallel at twelve knots, almost fifteen miles an hour.

Kathy stood on the port bridge wing, glancing frequently at the line that marked the distance separating the two vessels. The rope remained taut, the interval steady at eighty feet.

Less than an hour later, the addition of one hundred fifty thousand gallons of Diesel Fuel Marine topped off the ship's tanks.

"The oil king reports bunkers full, captain," she said to Taylor, the commanding officer (or CO), after a phone call from below. "Request permission to commence break-away."

The CO waved his hand. "Granted," he said.

Kathy stepped inside the pilothouse and picked up the handset for the UHF bridge-to-bridge radio telephone to the other ship, to halt the pumping.

Deck force sailors quickly disconnected the petroleum umbilical that linked the ships. Massive hoses slid back toward the tanker along tensioned steel wires. Lines splashed into the blue-green water of the Gulf Stream, hauled aboard by tanker crewmen as the last step in the fueling ended.

"Right standard rudder, come to course zero nine eight, make turns for twenty knots," Kathy ordered.

Two powerful gas turbine engines urged the single-propeller *Lockwood* smoothly forward into sunny, late-afternoon seas. Their forty-one-thousand-shaft horsepower could move the frigate at twenty-nine knots, almost thirty-five miles an hour, at top speed.

Kathy felt a thrill as her ship pulled away like an unfet-tered greyhound, it's bow throwing white water aside, pitching up and down and shuddering gently as it headed toward the setting sun. The lumbering oiler plodded along astern now, soon to turn east toward its next delivery. *Mer-rimack,* she recalled, was one of only two tankers in the fleet commanded by a woman.

Who wants to drive a fuel truck when you can tool around in a sports car? she said to herself. Her Uncle Gino, a retired destroyer commander, had first introduced her as a young girl to the small, fast ships that went in harm's way. Now she was proud both to be a ''tin can'' sailor and the first woman in her Naval Academy class to qualify as a Surface Warfare Officer in combatants. Over the next ten to fifteen years, Kathy thought, she'd prove to the Navy that she deserved command of one.

She remembered when her father had called her a stubborn fool for turning down Harvard for Annapolis. ''Be a surgeon. There's no money in sailing destroyers,'' he'd said, an argument he'd used with equal effect on his brother Eugene years before. Kathy knew there were more important things than money. Uncle Gino had introduced her to one of them.

The boatswain's pipe whistled again. ''Now secure the fueling detail, set the regular underway steaming watch. On deck, section two. The smoking lamp is lighted in all authorized spaces.'' The words echoed throughout the ship.

Salt breeze cooled her face with the change of course, and she began to relax. ''Great job, Petty Officer Thomas,'' Kathy said from the bridge wing. She spoke loudly enough so the captain and everyone else on the bridge knew the helmsman deserved credit. The eight women aboard during this mixed-manning experiment on a small vessel didn't get much of that, she thought.

Chapter Two

"Shannon, I would like to see you in my sea cabin when you come off watch."

When she looked at him, Commander Taylor's face was locked into a scowl as he slid off his bridge chair.

"Aye, aye, sir," she said, then took a deep breath. He was about to exercise the old Navy maxim of praising in public, criticizing in private again, she guessed.

An hour later, she tapped on the gray steel door of the captain's cabin and waited until he answered. He let her stand at attention for over a minute before he looked up from his paperwork and wheeled his chair around to face her. He did not offer her the other chair in the small, steel-walled room.

"Shannon, your maneuvers during this fueling were uncomfortably close."

The captain always called her by her last name, as enlisted people were addressed years ago, instead of by her rank. *He doesn't do that to other officers*, she noted to herself.

"Sir?"

6

"Eighty-foot distances between the tanker and us are too close. One hundred twenty feet would give us half again the room, and more time to act if we or the oiler had a steering breakdown requiring an emergency breakaway."

She had done the last one at one hundred feet, she thought, and he didn't complain.

"You may like to take chances, Shannon, but I do not, especially when it involves the safety of a hundred-million-dollar warship and my crew. It's not necessary to impress me with your seamanship, or how well Petty Officer Thomas can handle the helm. You should learn to use better judgment."

"I'll maintain one-hundred-twenty-foot interval in the future, Captain." If either ship had a rudder failure, the additional forty feet wouldn't have meant beans, she knew.

"I know you women are determined to prove yourselves, and that's fine. But don't do things that will risk my men or my ship. Understand?"

"But, sir, I—"

"Do you understand, Ms. Shannon?"

"Yes, sir."

"That will be all." The captain turned away from her and returned to his paperwork.

Kathy's face burned as she walked down the passageway toward the smallest stateroom on the ship. She couldn't very well share the junior officers' bunkroom and bath with a group of men. She wondered if Taylor was just picking on her again, or if he was worried about his next promotion in case anything went wrong during the refueling.

Nothing she did could please him. If she had made her fueling approach too wide, he'd have complained that it made it difficult for both ships to hook up and stay connected. A steering mechanism failure would have meant a burst of instant decisions for her, and quick moves for Petty Officer Thomas and the engineering watch, but the forty feet wouldn't have mattered. Even when she wrote letters for Taylor's signature she found them radically changed when they went out. *No point in arguing. When you're the captain, everyone does it your way*, she told herself.

"What's the matter, Kathy?" a soft southern voice said.

She looked up to see Lieutenant (jg) Roy Hobbs walking toward her, smiling. The sandy-haired Georgian was Main Propulsion Assistant in the ship's engineering department. He didn't wait for her to answer.

"That was a mighty smart UNREP you ran up there this afternoon," he said. "I watched it from the 01 level. Never saw a quicker approach or a cleaner breakaway."

"CO doesn't think so," she replied. "He says I was in too close. He wanted the distance at a hundred and twenty instead of eighty feet. Worth remembering if you do a fueling detail any time soon."

"How do *you* think it went, Kathy?" Hobbs's eyes appeared to seek hers. His voice carried a firm message now.

"Textbook. Close to perfect." She shrugged.

"Well, you're right, but you're too modest. It *was* one of the cleanest UNREPs I've ever seen. Wish I could do one as smoothly. You're a natural-born shiphandler. I wouldn't say that to make you feel good."

"Try telling the skipper," she said.

"As long as you know you did it right, that's what counts, shipmate." He patted her on the shoulder, then continued past her down the passageway. Strictly speaking, Roy wasn't supposed to touch her, but Roy Hobbs hadn't done anything he wouldn't do to any male colleague. His gesture was all right, and so was he.

Chapter Three

"Lieutenant Shannon, may I see you for a moment, please?"

The tap on her stateroom door had almost been swallowed by the noisy ventilation blower in the tiny living space. Kathy was doing sit-ups and push-ups before working on hull reports at her fold-up desk. The day after her chewing out by the captain, *Lockwood* steamed toward its first assignment on the drug interdiction line as part of the Atlantic Fleet's Western Hemisphere Group.

Instinct had told her shortly after reporting to the ship to do her exercise privately rather than out on the weather decks. A woman running around the deck in shorts would create more problems than it solved, she'd determined, especially after the ship had been at sea for more than a few days.

"Come on in," she said as she stood up.

When Kathy glanced up, she read anger on the young face of Quartermaster Third Class Susan Thomas.

"Come in, Susan; have a seat. What's the matter?"

"I . . . I don't know how to start this, or what I can do

9

about it. That's why I came to see you." Thomas's voice trembled.

"Don't worry, go ahead, any way you can." Kathy was prepared for any number of problems unique to women, none of them easily solved.

"My leading petty officer has been hitting on me. I've had to put him off some way almost every day for the past month. Today, he came after me."

"You mean QM1 Weatherby? He's married."

"I know. Even if he weren't, or wasn't my boss, I wouldn't date him. The man's a creep."

"What did he do?"

"I was pulling charts for our drug interdiction area in the chart house a few minutes ago. Suddenly, his hands were all over me. I'm so angry I could kill him." Susan Thomas's eyes blazed now.

"Did anyone else see him do this?"

"Weatherby's too smart for that, Lieutenant."

Kathy sighed. Her hand tightened into a fist. "What did you do, after he fondled you?"

"I cracked him as hard as I could, told him I'd kill him if he ever laid a hand on me again, and called him a couple of names."

"Good. What did he do then?"

"He laughed, said I couldn't take a joke."

"And no one saw, or heard, any of this, of course."

"No, ma'am, no one saw it." Thomas's eyes fell, her jaw set.

"To make your accusation stick, we need a witness, preferably a male witness, who'll testify against Weatherby."

"Isn't there something, anything, you can do?" The young enlisted woman sat with clenched fists. Her face showed a mixture of frustration and hope, Kathy thought.

"I'll talk to your division officer immediately, even the ops boss. We need to crack down on people like Weatherby. The other six women on the ship depend on that."

"Can you stop him, can any of us stop him?"

"We will. I'll make sure, for starters, that Weatherby can't mark you down on your performance Evaluation. Everyone 'knows sexual harassment isn't tolerated in the Navy, but some people never learn."

"What if he comes after me again?"

"I don't think he will after I talk to his boss and department head. If Weatherby's that foolish, kick him hard where it hurts, scream, make lots of noise, do whatever you have to. Then come see me immediately, any hour of the day or night. You don't have to tolerate this."

Thomas looked up, her eyes still smoldering with anger.

"Grab hold, sailor," Kathy said. "This is just another kind of fight. Women shouldn't have to worry about being safe among their own shipmates." She held a handful of tissue out to the young petty officer.

"Anyone ever tried this with you, Lieutenant?"

"Yes, but not here. The first one who does will find out what a third-degree black belt means."

"Wish I had one of those," Thomas said, socking her fist into her open hand.

"You shouldn't need one. No one should."

"Thanks for your help, Ms. Shannon. I know you'll do what's right." Susan got up to leave, stood taller, and dropped the tissues in the trash can.

"We'll beat this," Kathy said. "We have to."

Thomas nodded and closed the door quietly behind her.

Kathy sat at her desk, clenched her fist, then pounded one hard on the desk. She took a deep breath. She rose and pulled the ship's phone from its holder and cranked the number for the communications officer, who supervised the quartermasters and signalmen.

"Lieutenant (jg) Hartnett, please. This is Lieutenant (jg) Shannon."

A few seconds later, he was on the line.

"Gary, we have a problem. If you have a few minutes, I need to come up and see you."

"Can it wait until tomorrow, Kathy? I'm up to my ears right now."

"No, it can't. I'll scrub lunch, if you haven't any other time to do it. I need to see you now."

"That serious?"

"Yes, and timely. Has to be dealt with, like now."

"Okay, okay. How about in an hour, up here?"

"I'll be there," Kathy said.

She finished her reports, and then climbed the ladder to the communications shack an hour later. Kathy had purposely bought wash khaki uniform trousers and shirts a size larger than needed when she'd received orders to sea. She left her perfume ashore and wore only lipstick and some pressed powder, and sometimes not even that. No sense creating additional problems as one of eight women on a ship with two hundred men. Even if the numbers were even, she thought, mixed manning would be tough.

She opened the door to the communications office. Lieutenant (jg) Gary Hartnett sat amid a pile of publications and paper.

"Hi, Kathy," he said. "What's so hot that it can't wait?"

"Weatherby."

"What about him?"

"He's been sexually harassing Petty Officer Thomas. She put some bruises on him when he grabbed her this morning in the chart house. We have to stop this, Gary, and quick."

"Where did he grab her?"

"He had roaming hands. Places where men get cracked for fondling women. Not a pat on the shoulder."

"I suppose she has some proof."

"Now if you were Weatherby," Kathy replied, "would you go after a woman with a witness around?"

Hartnett sighed and pushed his chair back. "Kathy, how can I put Weatherby on report without proof? He's a married man. He also has a clean record up to now. A harassment charge means big trouble for him.''

''He should have thought of that before he messed with QM3 Thomas. Call him in, let him know that he's been reported.''

''Wait a minute. You haven't any proof and neither do I. This is her word against his.''

''Why would Thomas accuse him except for the obvious? She's a performer, your best helmsman, probably the sharpest enlisted navigator on the ship. Thomas is not some marginal sailor trying to 'get over.' ''

''Okay, okay, I'll call Weatherby in and get his side of the story.''

''No, Gary, call Weatherby in and tell him that if he lays a hand on Thomas again, he'll kiss his first-class crow, and maybe his career, good-bye. If you won't tell him that, send him to me, and I will. This isn't going to happen again. Not on this ship.''

''Now wait a minute, Kathy . . .''

''No, *you* wait a minute. You've never been messed with. You haven't the faintest idea of how soiled and damaged you feel after someone's pawed you. Another midshipman tried that on me at the Naval Academy. The mid ended up in the hospital for a week, and later became a civilian. Thomas doesn't have a karate belt. She shouldn't need one. If her shipmates and officers won't protect her, there's something very wrong with this Navy.''

The only sounds were the blowers and faint bleeps of computer equipment in the background. Kathy moved closer to Hartnett, fixing him with her eyes.

''Gary, if you won't correct this, and now, I will. I've got six other women who won't be safe if this turkey isn't stopped, and if the word gets around this kind of behavior is accepted . . .''

''Okay, okay. I'll bring Weatherby in and talk to him.''

''Tell him what I said. If he even touches Thomas again, he'll have a seabag full of trouble. If he's dumb enough to think a woman officer can't or won't slam-dunk him, he's going to learn quick.''

"No chance Thomas was exaggerating?''

"Not even close. Talk to her yourself. She can stand on her record, can't she?''

"Okay, she can stand on her record.''

"Thanks, Gary. I'll call you later to see how your session with Weatherby worked out. I'll let you tell the ops boss about this incident, too. No way this one's going to be swept under the rug.''

Hartnett rolled back in his chair, closed his eyes, and exhaled. He picked up the phone and rang the pilothouse. "I want to see Petty Officer Weatherby up here, on the double.''

"That's the spirit,'' Kathy said. She turned on her heel and walked through the door, pulling it shut behind her.

Chapter Four

Kathy felt perspiration under her arms as she shuffled quickly down the ship's ladder to the main deck. A knot of anger in her stomach, from Hartnett's reluctant reaction to the accusations against Weatherby, wouldn't go away.

She pushed open the watertight door to the weather deck and felt the cool salt breeze against her face. After she stepped out, Kathy pulled the steel door closed behind her, then walked forward to where her men worked near the missile launcher on the ship's bow. She was in charge of the ship's deck division, which maintained the weather, or outer, decks, and handled transfers like the refueling. Some deep breaths helped relieve the tension and funk of a few minutes earlier.

As she walked up, Boatswain's Mate First Class Harry Johnson, a tanned, lanky man, and Joe Ward, the ship's youthful, blond first-class electrician's mate, were bent over the anchor windlass control box. Johnson had told her that if they ever dropped anchor, he couldn't pull the ton of iron up until Ward fixed the motor controller.

"What's that controller problem look like?" she asked.

"Bad winding, or a saltwater leak shorted out the switches?"

"Ms. Shannon," Ward said, smiling, "you missed your calling. You should have been an electrician's mate."

"I had a hard enough time getting a job on a combatant ship as a officer," she replied. They all laughed.

"You're right about the corroded switch. How'd you know?" Ward asked.

"The electrician on the *Detroit* during my midshipman cruise repaired one and showed me how to do it."

"Hey, Ward," Johnson said, "Ms. Shannon *is* an electrician. But when they graduate folks from that high-priced trade school at Annapolis, they have to call them engineers." Johnson looked for a reaction, and saw Kathy smile.

"You broke the code again, Boats," she said as she strolled around the deck and breathed in the fresh air. When Johnson finished with the windlass problem, she walked over to him.

"QM1 Weatherby is about to find himself in a world of hurt, Boats. You might want him to know that."

Johnson looked uneasy. Her leading petty officer and the quartermaster were longtime acquaintances.

"What's the matter, Ms. Shannon?"

"He better keep his hands off the women. I can fix more than anchor windlasses. That's a serious warning for him. He won't get a second one."

Boats Johnson shifted around uncomfortably.

"You know that I really have two divisions on this ship, ours and the women. I'm going to do the best I can by both of them." She smiled and walked slowly away to where her other people repainted bulkheads farther aft, then went inside for lunch in the wardroom.

Lieutenant Commander Jeff Levine, the ship's executive officer, or XO, seemed an unlikely second-in-command on a warship. He was studious and of medium height, with thick glasses that made him appear bookish but couldn't conceal the keen intellect of an MIT-trained physicist. He'd go back ashore in a few months to a job at the Naval Research Lab in Washington, his other love. The skipper, Kathy thought, didn't seem to like Jeff any better than he liked her.

"XO, do you have a minute, sir?" she asked as lunch ended and everyone headed back to work.

"Sure, Kathy, come up and talk to me while I shuffle paperwork."

"It finally happened," she said.

Levine nodded. "Which one was it?" he asked.

"QM3 Thomas."

"Too bad. A very competent young woman. But that's not the point." Levine thought for a moment, then spoke again. "Let me guess. Weatherby?"

"How did you know, XO?"

"Weatherby is her boss, and he's too slick. He's had marital problems. Almost got locked up for spousal abuse a few months back. His wife's a nice gal . . . about Thomas's size. Of course, no witnesses, her word against his."

"Right," she said.

"Figures," Levine replied.

"If he messes with Petty Officer Thomas again, or any other woman on this ship, and it's not dealt with, for any reason including lack of witnesses, Weatherby will not, *repeat not,* get away with it," Kathy said softly.

Levine's expression when his eyes met hers told Kathy that he believed her.

"I'll have words with the skipper," he said. "I think Weatherby would make a very bad mistake to do this again."

As she walked back to her stateroom, Kathy was at least confident that Lieutenant Commander Levine was on her side.

The word should be out by now, she thought. She didn't start fights, but she would finish this one. If she didn't protect the women on this ship, no one would.

Chapter Five

Kathy awoke in the darkness with her hands locked onto the metal side rails of the bed in her stateroom. The chair by her desk clattered to the floor and slammed up against the iron door, as the ship heeled hard into what had to be an emergency turn to port. *Lockwood* stayed heeled over for several seconds, like a sailboat on a breezy day, then snapped upright. When the ship stabilized, Kathy sat up and punched the night-glow button on her watch. 0315. What the heck had happened?

She stumbled to her locker in the dull red glow of a night lamp, pulled on a khaki shirt and pants, and slid bare feet into work shoes. Then she hurried forward up the darkened passageway toward the ladder to the bridge.

When Kathy reached the pilothouse, the captain and XO were there, the CO in his blue bathrobe, the XO in khaki pants and an undershirt with shower shoes. A chilly night wind blew in from the steel doors to the bridge wings. Taylor grilled Lieutenant (jg) Hobbs, the officer of the deck, about the abrupt course change.

"Tanker bears 020, estimate 2,500 yards, opening range,

18

maintaining steady bearing,'' the quartermaster cried out from the port bridge wing.

''Very well,'' Hobbs acknowledged, then returned to his conversation with the ship's two senior officers.

''What do you mean, the radar showed that tanker at twelve thousand yards only a minute before you made this emergency turn?'' Taylor bellowed, his hair askew.

''Captain, take a look. You can see his lights off the port bow, and here's where the radar says he is, six miles away. If our starboard lookout hadn't spotted the tanker's running lights, we wouldn't have known he was there. We're out of the shipping lanes. That merchant was probably on the Iron Mike, with nobody watching their radar. Our own surface search is badly out of whack.''

Not the first time she'd seen a merchant ship run on automated steering in an area where they expected no ships, Kathy thought.

''The tanker's riding high, so she's empty, probably barreling back for another cargo,'' Roy added.

Kathy went to the radar repeater, flipped the range switches from long to medium to short, and examined the other adjustments. While the CO continued to interrogate Roy, she walked to the other side of the pilothouse and examined the second bridge repeater.

''The problem's not in our repeaters,'' she said, referring to the local radar displays. ''It's in the main ranging circuitry. Not calibration, either. Whatever broke down failed in the last few hours. This radar worked fine when I had the watch between six and eight last evening.''

Taylor threw her a who-asked-you glance, his face sour and in need of a shave. The operations officer stepped through the pilothouse door, buttoning his shirt.

''Ops, get your ETs working on this radar ASAP,'' the skipper said. ''If we don't have it up in the next two days, we're useless on the drug interdiction line. We'll be sent home to fix it, and I don't want that, understand?''

''Yes, sir. In the meantime,'' the ops boss said, ''I'll

double up the lookouts until after sunrise to give us more eyes on the horizon.''

''Make it so. Meanwhile, Mr. Hobbs, kindly get us back on course and make the appropriate log entries. Ops, send a CASREP message on the surface search saying we initially evaluate the radar problem as a ship's force repair. Can your electronic genius McCloud fix this one?''

The operations officer exhaled tiredly. He didn't need to be told to file a casualty report, Kathy thought, and had no idea whether McCloud could fix the radar or not.

''I don't know, Cap'n. He's handled some tough ones since the chief ET transferred out. We'll get him on it first thing. If Kathy's right, we have a larger problem than the repeaters.''

''Ms. Shannon is *not* an electronics technician,'' Taylor growled, ''and hasn't been to advanced Radar 'B' school, as far as I know. Have McCloud check *everything.*''

Kathy felt her face flush, but no one could see that, or her tightly clenched fist, in the dark pilothouse. *So much for being helpful. Should have kept my mouth shut*, she admonished herself.

When the CO left, she walked up to the operations officer, Lieutenant Steve Hearst. ''We had a similar problem on the Coast Guard cutter I rode during my exchange tour,'' she said. ''This is a more complex system, but the problem isn't the repeaters. Our Coast Guard ET put on a fix that wasn't in the book and we stayed on station. If I can help McCloud, let me know. No need to tell the old man.''

Hearst nodded.

He wouldn't ask her unless they were desperate, Kathy thought. She returned to her stateroom, draped the uniform over a chair, and climbed back under the covers. If those lookouts hadn't spotted the tanker's running lights, and Roy hadn't acted so decisively, the massive merchant ship would have cut them in two, killing dozens of sailors, perhaps including her. She shuddered. *I must compliment Roy for his seamanship, even though the old man didn't. Why am I not surprised?*

When Kathy came off the forenoon watch at 1145 and entered the wardroom for lunch, a long-faced Steve Hearst told her about the radar.

"You were right," he said. "McCloud ruled out the repeaters in fifteen minutes. The main circuitry has been driving him bonkers ever since. He troubleshot all the standard-stock problems. No joy yet."

"The skipper doesn't want to hear that," she said.

"He'll eat me and McCloud for supper if we're ordered off the drug line to fix a busted radar."

"My offer is still good," Kathy said. "I'm no expert, but I know circuit architecture and remember the problems we fixed on that cutter."

"Can't hurt. I'll tell him you'll come down this afternoon. Thanks, Kathy. This one's not your problem. I owe you one."

"Any problem I can fix on this ship is my problem," she said. *I'll call in this marker if Weatherby ever lays hands on Thomas again*, she mentally noted.

A half hour later, Kathy and Electronics Technician Second Class Gary McCloud sat on the steel deck of the cramped compartment full of electronics, including the surface-search radar circuitry. Schematics and manufacturers' instruction binders covered the floor.

"Pass me that flashlight, please," she asked McCloud. She crowded her head in between the console and the bulkhead, slowly playing the light along rows of circuit boards. The eyeball check was a long shot. The hard part, yet to come, required precision test instruments.

"How'd you get in the radar repair game, Ms. Shannon?" McCloud asked. "Most officers don't know zip about electronics."

"When I was on exchange duty with the Coast Guard,

our ET had a problem like this. Between his knowledge of radars and what I knew about circuit design, we isolated the problem and patched it. Maybe we can do that here.''

"Find anything?" McCloud's voice sounded muffled. He scanned the other side of the equipment.

"Not yet. Sure this is all the ranging circuitry?"

"That's what the book says. Some of these repairs are not ship's force jobs, require a manufacturer's tech rep, or the shipyard. I have a locker full of circuit boards and black box spares, but the main circuits all check out with the test gear. This radar ought to be working fine. Should I run all the system checks again?"

"No, I'm sure you did them right the first time," she said, smiling at him.

The blue-eyed, tousle-haired ET was about her height, very bright and easygoing. His eyes engaged hers when he spoke to her, his smile warm. Kathy felt comfortable around him.

For two hours, they pored over diagrams, tested circuits, and crawled in to check cables and connections that might have shaken loose from the ship's relentless vibration. Several times, his elbow brushed against her, or his warm breath reached her neck as they crowded into tight spaces together.

"Sorry," he muttered, ". . . cramped in here."

"No problem," she said. "Let's get the job done."

After two fruitless hours, the two sat quietly on the deck amid stacks of books and electronic test gear.

"Are you thinking what I'm thinking?" she asked.

"You mean pull it apart board by board, test every circuit? That'll take two days, minimum."

"If you have a better idea, we'll try that first. Besides, we don't have two days. The ship arrives on station day after tomorrow, and we need this gear running before then."

"You're right." He breathed deeply. "Maybe we better get started."

"I'll swap off my 20–24 watch tonight, and be back in a few minutes."

After agreeing to exchange her 8:00 P.M. to midnight watch for a midnight to 4:00 A.M. watch later, Kathy returned to the radar console space. The bad deal was all she could work out on short notice.

"You don't have to do this," he said. "This radar isn't your problem. If Chief Reeves were still here, he and I would . . ."

"But he's not here," she said. "Now if we know enough electronics between us to fix a radar, and I think we do, let's start pulling circuit boards."

McCloud smiled, a little more warmly this time.

At eight that night, Lieutenant Commander Levine looked in and saw circuit boards and test equipment everywhere. The XO rolled his eyes and groaned.

"Oy," he muttered.

"Nah, XO, not nearly as bad as it looks," McCloud said. "The crunch comes when we find the bum circuit board. If we don't have a spare or can't get one from a nearby ship, we can all start sweating."

Levine's eyes flitted to Kathy.

"Petty Officer McCloud has it right, XO," she said.

"How long?" Levine asked.

"All night, at least, maybe longer," McCloud replied.

He looked at Kathy again.

She nodded. "More like 'maybe longer,' I think."

"I'll get your deck watches re-rigged, Kathy."

"I already fixed tonight, sir," she said.

"I know. You didn't have to buy that mid-watch while you're on an emergency project. I would have fixed it."

She shrugged. "I volunteered for this."

"Thanks, Kathy," the XO said as he pulled the door closed. "Good luck on getting this thing fixed, you two."

About 11:30 P.M., McCloud stood up and stretched.

"This kid needs some coffee. Can I get you some from the mess decks, Lieutenant? How do you like it?"

"Black and bitter, thanks." When Kathy stood up, a cramp pained her right leg. Tiredness washed over her after hours of meticulous circuit checks. They should have taken a break long ago.

She headed back to her stateroom. As she freshened up, Kathy wished she could climb into bed and sleep.

As she returned, she saw McCloud walking slowly down the dark passageway, balancing two cups of coffee. He offered her one and they climbed down to the equipment space through a berthing compartment full of sleeping male sailors. The muddy, bitter brew, Kathy reckoned, had been made about six hours earlier. The stuff tasted like boiled tennis shoes.

"What brought you into the Navy?" she asked McCloud.

"Ran out of money in college. Unexpected financial crisis when my kid sister needed surgery. There was no scholarship money available at mid-year."

"What college?"

"Studied electrical engineering at RIT in Rochester. Two and a half years. The recruiters jumped to offer me Third Class Petty Officer when I completed ET 'A' school."

One of the best engineering schools in the country, she thought. No wonder he was so sharp.

After coffee, they returned to the tedious testing. A few times, his hand brushed hers. They talked as they worked through the night. When Gary went up to the mess decks for more coffee at 3:00 A.M., she stretched and contemplated how attractive he was. Then she brushed the idea from her mind. Regulations made any enlisted man strictly off limits.

At six-thirty in the morning, the door to the electronics compartment swung open. Commander Taylor looked in, his face stern. He stared past Kathy as though she weren't there. "Can you fix this radar, McCloud?"

Gary paused before he answered.

"Ms. Shannon and I are doing our best, Captain, but we don't know yet. If it can be fixed at sea, *we* will fix it . . . sir."

Taylor hesitated for a second.

"Okay, keep me informed," he said, and pulled the door closed.

"I didn't realize the skipper had a vision problem," McCloud said. "He didn't even seem to see you."

"Too bad." She shrugged. "Glad I don't have one."

"Well, I'm seeing double," McCloud said. "We should catch a few hours of Zs before we start making mistakes, and then come back again after lunch. If we find that bad circuit at all, we'll catch it in the next three or four hours of testing. What do you think?"

"Yes," Kathy replied, "but this time tomorrow, we're supposed to be on station. By then, we have to locate the problem, find a replacement, install it, burn it in, and test the system. We don't have much time."

"I couldn't finish on time at all, without you," McCloud said, his voice softer now.

Before she knew it, he had taken her hand in both of his and squeezed it lightly. The gesture was that of a man expressing affection. She'd felt it before. His eyes said other things as well. *Careful, Kathy,* she warned herself.

"Don't thank me," she said. "We're not nearly finished yet. I agree with you about those Zs." Kathy gently withdrew her hand to cover her mouth as she yawned. "See you around 1300."

On the way back to her stateroom, she stopped to see Lieutenant Commander Levine.

"We'll know in a few hours, XO, but right now, I have to crash."

"Old man's really uptight, you know."

"Tell me about it," she said. "He came by for a social call at 0630, even before he'd eaten his first box of nails."

Levine tried, without success, to suppress a smile.

After five hours of restless sleep, Kathy returned to the

tiny space. McCloud was already there. The seas had picked up. The ship pitched and rolled in growing swells from a passing rain squall. It was harder to stand up, she thought, and easier to become seasick down there where it was warm.

At 2000, 8:00 P.M., after a quick meal and several cups of coffee, McCloud wrinkled up his face and said "Hmm."

"What did you find, Gary?" she said, realizing only then that she'd used his first name. He looked directly at her. Maybe that was a mistake.

"Low reading on this one, low and unsteady," he said. "Maybe, just maybe, a weak component. Here, you test it."

"Why wouldn't that show up on your original trouble-shoot?" She took the circuit and the tester from him.

"Because it's marginal, perhaps strong enough to pass, but too weak or unstable to do the job. May not be this circuit at all. May be a combination of two or more bad ones."

"A couple of ways to go," she said. "See if we have a spare circuit board, plug it in, and go. Otherwise, we check the rest, then come back to this. That would also validate your theory about more than one bad circuit."

"It'll only take an hour to test the rest of them," he said. "Then we'll be sure. Let's go for it. We can really run up the overtime tab on this job." McCloud laughed.

"I can see you haven't read the fine print in your contract. I'd settle for an afternoon off," she said.

"I'll take one day of ropeyarning and call it even," he said.

An hour later, McCloud discovered another problem. At least they'd found the bad one . . . maybe. He sat with the bad board in one hand, heaved a long sigh, and hung his head down.

"It would be one we don't have a spare for," he said, tired now.

"Do you have spec sheets on these circuit boards?" Kathy asked.

"You mean like the bad one?"

"I mean like all of them, including the bad one," she said.

"You mean find a spare that's close, and adapt it?"

"Adapt it, cannibalize it, patch it with chewing gum, whatever works," she said.

"That'll violate NAVSEA doctrine," he said, "but who cares, if a jury-rigged circuit gets the radar up."

"That's all the skipper cares about right now," she said. "Why not order the replacement with a PRI ONE logistic message, then plug it in when we get it. If you find one to modify for now, no one will ask questions. Get this radar up and you're a hero."

"If the jury-rigged one doesn't blow the whole system," he said. "You're talking about taking a fifty-thousand-dollar chance, Ms. Shannon, maybe more."

"Just how good are we?" she said. "Besides, they always hang the officers." She laughed, but knew the old man would hang *her* if an unauthorized repair caused major damage.

"We've come this far bending the rules," he said, looking her in the eye.

After poring through the specifications for circuit boards, her eyes felt bleary, scratchy. She looked at the printed list and circled a number.

"See if you have one of these," she said, pointing to a page in the manufacturer's manual.

"This board has no redundancy, no backup circuit," he said. "If it blows, this gear is down again, suddenly and hard . . . like dead."

McCloud examined the two spec sheets. "I'll have to disconnect another circuit on this board first, or it'll screw up the image on the repeater screens. But you're right, this gizmo could work."

He helped her up again, his arms strong, his eyes confident.

McCloud returned twenty minutes later with a silver-plastic electronics part bag. "Do you want the good news or the bad news first?" he asked.

"The bad news, of course."

"This little stinker costs three thousand bucks."

"So . . . what's the good news?" she asked.

"That we had it on board. The other bad news is that it's the only one. If we light off and it goes south, that's the ball game. We're back into port and the old man will turn us into barbecue."

"No guts, no glory, shipmate," Kathy said.

"True. I'll modify this and we'll crank it up. I'm ready for a good night's sleep."

"I'll get permission from the OOD to radiate the surface search for a test. Never thought I'd look forward to some rest so darn much."

"Sleep lightly," he said. "You know the most likely fail time on new circuit boards is when they're burning in. If this thing makes it past the first five to ten hours, chances are we're home free."

She walked out to call the bridge, and returned a few minutes later. McCloud was finishing his modification to the circuit board with a soldering iron and needle-nosed pliers.

"We're cleared to radiate," she said.

Twenty minutes later, at three minutes after two in the morning, the SPS-55 surface-search radar of the USS *Lockwood* was up and running again. They went to the ops center, then to the bridge, and checked each repeater. The picture looked perfect.

"We did it, shipmate," McCloud said as they stood a few minutes later in the narrow, darkened passageway below the bridge. Gary was an electronics expert who just happened to be a sailor, she thought. He wouldn't stay in the Navy, probably didn't even want to understand certain hard things about the way the Navy had to work. In another couple of years, he'd be out, finishing his degree in electrical engineering.

"Sure does," she replied. "You did a great job."

"No," he said, moving closer and taking her hand again, "*we* did a great job. Not only that, we're so modest about it."

Both laughed, and she withdrew her hand gently.

"Good night . . . Gary. I have to get some sleep before I nod off standing up."

By 0300 Kathy slid between the covers of her bunk. Another short night. Today the ship would take up station in a new area assigned to the drug interdiction task force. In a few days, she knew a team of Coast Guard enlisted men called a LEDET or Law Enforcement Detachment would embark to join the Coast Guard officer they'd brought out with them. The Coast Guardsmen would board any suspicious vessels under the cover of Navy guns and the *Lockwood*'s helicopter.

Chapter Six

"Kathy, come up and see me when you have a minute. Not urgent. Any time today."

The XO's voice on her stateroom phone sounded tired. Lieutenant Commander Levine had been under strain since the ship arrived on the drug interdiction line, a first assignment of that type. Only Kathy had previous experience. Her exchange tour with the Coast Guard taught her about stopping and boarding suspicious vessels.

"Is 1000 okay for you, XO?" she said.

"Sure, Kathy," he said, "whenever it's convenient for you."

She walked into Levine's office an hour later. He offered her a seat, and looked pensive. "The CO has approved a Navy Achievement Medal for the great job done in repairing the surface-search radar under difficult circumstances."

"You said *a* medal, XO. Does that mean one? Who's it for?" She knew her words sounded guarded.

"Yes, that means one." Levine's head dipped, his lips pursed. "He left it to me to decide who gets it."

Isn't that lovely, she thought wryly.

"You recommended two, didn't you?" she asked.

The executive officer avoided her eyes.

"What I recommended doesn't matter. What we have is one medal for two deserving people. You would have taken the blame if that radar burned up, if your fix didn't work. You hung out a mile on this one. I want you to have it."

Kathy drew her breath in slowly and exhaled.

"ET2 McCloud would have figured out how to make the repair by himself."

"You're too modest," the XO said. "He wouldn't have fixed it *in time* without you. We would have reported to the drug interdiction line with a major equipment casualty."

"Perhaps he would have finished on time alone," she said.

"No perhaps," he said. "I saw you two tear that radar apart, remember? How even both of you got that gear repaired in a day and a half is well near incredible."

"I know what you're saying, XO, and I appreciate your feelings. If you're asking me, I want you to give the medal to Petty Officer McCloud."

Levine nodded. She knew now why he sounded tired. He really had pushed the captain for two awards.

"Kathy, this one is your call, and I won't argue with you. Either way you'd be correct."

"But this way is a little more right, isn't it?"

"It tells your shipmates a lot about you," he replied.

"That's not why I'm doing it."

"I know, I know," he said softly, raising his hands. "Thanks, Kathy."

"Thank you for asking me, XO. Many people wouldn't. If that's all, sir . . ."

She stood to leave, and reached for the door handle.

"Kathy?"

She looked back toward him.

"Sometimes it's tough to be a really good officer."

"Thanks, XO."

As she walked back to her stateroom, Kathy knew she probably wouldn't get that afternoon off, either.

Chapter Seven

Kathy labored over a series of weekly hull reports in the tiny Weapons Department office. A knock on the door distracted her.

"Come in." She didn't look up immediately from the computer on which she completed inspection forms on spaces under her charge. The reports were late, so she concentrated on them for a few more seconds.

"I didn't mean to interrupt you," he said. When she looked up, the lean tallness of Electronics Technician Second Class Gary McCloud stood only feet from her. She felt warmth rising in her face.

"I'm sorry," she replied. She smiled sheepishly at him and stood up. "I didn't mean to keep you waiting. These reports are almost overdue, and that's my fault."

"I know you gave up that Navy Achievement Medal so they'd award it to me," he said. "You'd have taken the blame if we failed. Giving up that medal was a really kind thing to do."

"You deserved the award," she said.

"I don't quite know how to put this," he said, "and

forgive me if I don't get it right. You're the most intelligent, attractive lady I've met in a long time . . . perhaps ever. Would you have dinner with me one evening when we get back into port?''

Kathy agonized, hesitating as she selected her words. *I don't want to hurt him, but there's no other way,* she thought sadly.

She turned toward him. His eyes engaged hers intensely.

''Thank you. I'm flattered,'' she said softly, lowering her eyes. Gary's had the hopeful desperation of a man on the edge of love. When she looked up, she knew her face looked pained. She intended that. *Here goes,* she told herself.

''But I can't. You're a wonderful person, and I regard you highly, but I can't go out with you. Navy regulations bind me even more tightly than they do you.''

She hesitated. ''None of us can—'' Without warning, Gary McCloud reached over and kissed her. His lips were warm. She started to pull back.

''Gary—''

He silenced her again with a warmer, even more ardent kiss. She liked it, as she had the first one.

''Gary, you must stop now . . . please.''

''I meant everything that goes with that, Kathy,'' he whispered. His voice was soft; his arms had been inviting. The whole thing was impossible.

''You haven't known me long enough or well enough to care for me that much. Strange things happen to men and women at sea for weeks at a time.''

''Those are normal things, natural things,'' he replied.

''Maybe in the rest of the world,'' she replied, ''but not on a Navy warship.''

She hesitated for only a second.

''Gary, I admire you and think you're a wonderful person, but . . .''

''You have someone else,'' he said.

''Yes,'' she fibbed. ''Yes, I do.'' But her occasional

dates with Dr. Dana Mansfield weren't what McCloud meant. She felt a hard twinge in the pit of her stomach. *Giving up the medal was easy compared with this.*

"I'm sorry. I didn't mean to hassle you," he said. His eyes dropped.

"You'll make the right woman very happy. Sometimes things aren't meant to be. I'm sorry."

He took her hand, squeezed it gently, and kissed her ever so lightly on the forehead.

She heard him sigh, although he probably hadn't intended it to be heard.

"I guess I have to get back to the Navy," he said.

"I think we both do," she replied.

"Right, Lieutenant. I guess we all learn by living."

"But not all the lessons are what we expect," she said.

Gary smiled grimly as he pulled the door shut behind him. The only sound in the steel-walled, gray compartment was the endless hum of the blower. She felt a tear at the corner of her left eye, brushed it away, and turned back to the computer.

Chapter Eight

August breezes blowing gently across *Lockwood*'s bow made the Caribbean morning delightful. Kathy stood on the fo'c'sle and recalled she hadn't seen such beautiful cloud formations since she'd sailed down here with the Coast Guard a year earlier.

Kathy yawned. She'd been up since 0330, when she'd awakened for the morning watch. After a quick breakfast, she walked around the deck for exercise.

The XO had said in the wardroom that she was today's duty boarding officer if the skipper ordered inspection of a suspicious ship. A Coast Guard lieutenant, who had law enforcement authority the Navy didn't, performed all boardings as the U.S. representative, with an armed Navy backup. They were stretched thin on the drug patrol, Kathy knew, and the Coast Guard welcomed help from the organization they'd long referred to without malice as "big brother."

When she returned to her stateroom, Kathy felt tired. Must have been those seventeen-hour days this past week. A staggered watch schedule kept her on the bridge for a different eight hours each day. You took sleep when you could get it. She decided to steal some now.

Drug interdiction had been boring so far. Other ships had reported surface contacts and inspections of suspicious vessels, but nothing had yet come *Lockwood*'s way.

She'd only been asleep for minutes, she thought, when the ship's telephone circuit *whoop-whooped* a few feet away. "We have a suspicious small merchant in sight, Kathy," the XO said. "We'll call away the boarding party shortly. Thought you'd want to check out your boat crew."

Kathy brushed sleep from her eyes, splashed water on her face, and freshened up. *The pistol,* she thought, *check out the pistol.* She'd learned from her Coast Guard tour to expect anything upon boarding a vessel that stopped only because Navy or Coast Guard guns were aimed at it.

Kathy kept a pistol belt in the ship's small armory. She always cleaned the .45-caliber pistol herself and loaded her own clips. The Navy wouldn't convert to the more modern and powerful 9mm Beretta pistol for another couple of years, she'd heard. Unlike many Regular Navy members, she took sidearms and the Landing Party Manual seriously, and practiced marksmanship regularly after her exchange tour with the Coast Guard. If fired upon out here, she knew she must be prepared to shoot back accurately, or die. An unpleasant reality, she thought.

As she left her stateroom, the piercing trill of the boatswain's whistle preceded a call over the ship's announcing system. *"Now all boarding party report to the motor whaleboat. Draw small arms and flak jackets from the gunner's mate at ship's armory. Stand by to lower away in ten minutes."*

When she stepped out on deck, she saw the striped flag of the Coast Guard fluttering in the breeze. All boardings were done under that service's law enforcement authority.

Minutes later, Kathy strapped on the pistol belt with extra clips. She drew the weapon, pointed it over the side, and pulled back the slide, working the action. After she loaded a clip into it, Kathy slid the heavy pistol into its holster and went to inspect the armed men who'd accompany her, and check in with the Coast Guard rep who'd lead the boarding party.

Target practice for most of the men had consisted of shooting from the fantail at cans and similar objects in the ship's wake. As far as she knew, none of them, herself included, had ever shot at a human being. She continued to hope she wouldn't have to.

Lieutenant Jack Goldhaver, the Coast Guard officer riding the ship, was a large, gregarious man who admitted to difficulty traversing narrow passageways on his service's smaller cutters. Known good-naturedly as "The Hulk," Goldhaver skirted the Coast Guard's upper limits for height and weight. He wore a badge which indicated he'd previously commanded a cutter.

As they stood on deck, *Lockwood* completed a high-speed circle around the smaller vessel. A very clear way to tell them there was no escape, no sense making a run for it, she thought.

"Here we go again," Goldhaver said, smiling at her. He had remarkably good humor after so many boardings. Most, she knew, involved tedious document checks and fruitless crawling through musty freighter holds.

"Better than riding the subway to work," he said as they waited on the deck, which reminded her he was also from New York.

"Right," she replied. "Maybe even more exciting."

He checked his own pistol. "Not if you've been back home lately. One of these would come in handy back there."

"Why do you think I'm here?" she said dryly. "I wanted a nice safe job outside Manhattan."

"Sure," he replied wryly, plugging his handgun into its holster. "So here you are. What could be safer than this?"

Kathy checked out the boarding party before they stepped into the whaleboat suspended from the ship's port side. The men, dressed in dungaree shirts and trousers, wore bulky bulletproof flak jackets and carried M-14 rifles with ammunition belts clasped around their waists. Gray painted steel helmets replaced blue ball caps.

The *Lockwood* had moved within a few hundred yards of the freighter and seemed to purposely dominate the smaller ship with its larger, armed presence.

As deck seamen lowered away the twenty-six-foot motor whaleboat filled with armed sailors, Kathy studied the rusty coastal freighter, the *Marialena*. Less than three hundred feet long, she gauged, the old ship was built low to the water. No wonder they'd stopped it. Designed for coastal commerce, the vessel looked out of place on the high seas this far from home. The Panamanian flag flew from the freighter's foretruck, but revealed nothing of where it had most recently made port.

The coastal had stopped after a radioed order to "heave to" by a Spanish-speaking *Lockwood* crewmember, Petty Officer Juan Torres. Probably another routine examination of papers, Kathy thought, but never a job to take lightly. Part of their mission, she knew, was to show American determination to make the drug trade difficult and dangerous for smugglers. She looked up and saw *Lockwood*'s LAMPS helicopter orbiting in a wide circle overhead.

As their bouncing boat approached the freighter's accommodation ladder, Kathy saw what appeared to be a lot of activity on the main deck, with people rushing around, especially near the cargo hatches. A scruffy crewman with a cigarette hanging from his mouth glared at them from the deck with a vicious stare. The back of Kathy's neck tingled.

"Jack!" she said.

"Yeah," he replied as he looked up from checking the paperwork in his boarding package.

"Careful with this one."

"You worry too much, Kathy."

"I'm telling you, watch it this time."

"Okay, okay," he said as the boat bobbed toward the ship's port side.

Goldhaver jumped up on the platform as the boat found the crest of a wave. He lashed the bowline to the ladder. Kathy clambered off after him. Her tense tingle continued as Jack climbed toward the deck. Gunner's Mate First Class Sam Apriliou was behind her. As she neared the top she turned to him.

"Gunner, I don't like this one. Have the men lock and load. Fan out quickly as soon as we cross their quarterdeck."

"Aye, aye, ma'am," he replied, then turned and gave hand signals to the six men behind him. Kathy heard breeches snap shut on six service rifles, as the sailors climbed the last few steps. She hoped the men had learned well from their target practice.

An unshaven, skinny Latino with a rumpled, dirty maritime officer's cap waited at the top of the ladder. He smiled at Goldhaver through missing teeth.

As a shark smiles, Kathy thought, scanning the low, flat deck of the freighter, her stomach tense. She stepped quickly aside to let her armed boarding party deploy. For all the frantic activity of a few minutes before, four freighter crewmen now seemed to lounge around twenty feet away near the cargo hatches, talking and watching. *Something doesn't look right,* she told herself.

Suddenly, she felt vibration under her feet, as though the ship's engines had started. These idiots were trying to make a run for it. Jack was examining the ship's papers and cargo manifest with the ship's captain and a bilingual American sailor. He must have looked up when he felt the vibration, too. She glanced around in time to see a flash from the direction of one man who'd been standing around.

Pop! Pop!

That was a gun in his hand!

"Take cover!" she shouted as she drew her pistol and dropped to one knee behind the forward cargo hatch. Her men scrambled behind the raised hatch covers as more bullets whined off the nearby metal. She winced as she saw Jack spin and fall, and the scruffy Latino captain turn to flee.

Within seconds, she'd punched out half a clip toward the armed man who'd shot at Jack. The others had disappeared and were firing from someplace else. *Pow! Pow! Pow! Pow!* Her powerful pistol roared; her ears rang, and the muzzle jumped as it recoiled. Jack's assailant dropped from sight.

Kathy launched herself toward the fleeing captain and tackled him. By the time they hit the deck, another sailor who must have seen the man break away landed on top of them.

"He's yours, Briggs," she said to the young petty officer. "If he moves, *muerto*." She drew her hand across her throat. The smuggler flinched, his eyes wide.

Ricochets pinged off the thick steel shell plating of the freighter's deck all around her. Sailors crouched, then jumped up to pour bursts of rifle fire at smuggler crewmen who had them pinned down. When several close rounds pinged inches from her head, a cold quiver of mortal fear paralyzed her for a few seconds. *Got to get moving,* she admonished herself.

Jack Goldhaver lay facedown, motionless. Everything had happened within thirty seconds.

Dear God, no, Kathy prayed silently.

"Corpsman!" she shouted. The *Lockwood*'s junior medic, Hospitalman Third Class Bernadette Fiori, crawled forward awkwardly from her refuge on the accommodation ladder. Fiori had no weapon.

Kathy turned to Apriliou about ten feet away. The older man carried the portable radio transceiver.

"Gunner, call for backup, then take two men and secure the bridge. Take no chances. Shoot any armed resistance. No more of my sailors get wounded by these turkeys."

Goldhaver moaned as the hundred-pound female

corpsman struggled to turn him over. A widening circle of blood oozed through his khaki shirt. Jack should have zipped up that flak jacket, Kathy thought.

She crawled quickly across the deck toward him. "Jack?" Kathy asked.

"I'm okay . . . take charge. I'll join you when the corpsman patches me up," Goldhaver said groggily.

He was in shock, half-conscious.

" 'Doc,' fix up Mr. Goldhaver, and keep him from catching any more bullets, please," Kathy snapped.

The petite, raven-haired, nineteen-year-old slipped the canvas medical kit from her shoulder. Without hesitation, she pulled Jack's pistol from its holster, cranked a round into the chamber, and set the weapon on the deck beside her.

"Gotcha, Ms. Shannon. I'll take care of him," Fiori said.

Kathy thrust a raised thumb in the corpsman's direction.

"Jack," she said, "you've deputized me to arrest this crew, and to confiscate this ship on behalf of the U.S. government, right?"

"Of course. Why are you sitting here talking about it?" he whispered. His grimace told her the bullet hurt.

Kathy heard a burst of fire and the tinkling smash of glass from the bridge area. The two sailors near her ducked, then scanned the decks for other armed men, punching out rounds to cover themselves as they looked.

"You have that bridge secured, Gunner?" she shouted.

"Yeah, Ms. Shannon, these guys aren't goin' anywhere."

The gunfire suddenly stopped.

"I'll be up in a few minutes."

"Let's go," she said to two nearby seamen. "We'll find the engine room and stop this rustbucket."

As Kathy rushed aft, she wished Roy Hobbs were here. He'd know more about what to do in an engine room, how to stop everything, keep them from opening scuttle valves to sink the ship and destroy evidence.

Suddenly, she heard a loud crack. A shot whistled across the bow of the freighter. The three-inch round from the midships gun on *Lockwood* told the smugglers to stop or be taken under fire. Psychological, she thought. The ship knew from the gunner's radio message that they were slugging it out with the druggies.

Kathy's heart pounded now, her mouth dry. The two young sailors behind her looked pasty white, their eyes wide. When they came to a door on the side of the main deck, she waved them back. She reached for the door with her left hand, stood back with the pistol in her right, and flipped it open.

Nothing happened.

She jumped through the opening, swept the .45 through a wide arc, and smelled hot oil and steam. The ladder to her left must lead down to the ship's engine room.

"Follow me," she ordered, and clambered down the metal stairs into the engineering space, more like a steam room. The two crewmen were startled to see an American officer, Kathy thought, especially a woman officer. Neither appeared armed.

"Stop the engines, now!" she roared at the two, then remembered who they were. She struggled to remember her Spanish. *"¡Alto la máquina! Ahora!"* Kathy shouted over the hissing noise of the engines. Kathy pointed her pistol at the head of the larger of the two, and felt her arm tremble slightly. The crewman who disappeared after she shot at him minutes earlier had jangled her nerves. The men seemed confused; they didn't seem to know whether she wanted them to halt what they were doing, or to stop the engines. They raised their hands. *Wish I'd taken Spanish instead of German at Annapolis,* she told herself.

"¡Alto la máquina, ahora, ahora!" she repeated clearly, as she rushed toward the larger man and poked the pistol under his chin. Her eyes flashed. The two armed sailors covered her now, rifles at the ready. One smuggler pointed to the control valves.

Kathy waved the pistol. The wide-eyed, sweating crewman quickly spun closed the main steam valve to the engines.

"Down . . . *¡abajo, abajo!*" she shouted. The two men hurried to lie facedown on the steel deck plates.

She turned to the husky black sailor behind her. "You're in charge here, Petty Officer Rash. Tie 'em up. If anyone comes toward you, drill him." She turned to the two smugglers and said, *"Una problema y muerto,"* and again drew her hand across her throat. Even the most macho smugglers, she reckoned, had enough sense to fear the word that could end their lives.

Kathy left the two sailors in the engine room, and charged up the ladder to check on Goldhaver.

Fiori had torn off most of Jack's shirt, and now bent over him to clean the messy, heavily bleeding puncture. The wound below his left shoulder was more serious, or at least bloodier, than Goldhaver had admitted. He sat with his back propped against the steel bulkhead, the pistol now in his right hand. His eyes scanned the main deck while Fiori worked quickly to patch him up. Her back faced the action. Perspiration glistened on her face despite the cool breeze.

Kathy watched Bernadette Fiori, a woman only a year out of high school, who had taken Jack's weapon, ready to shoot the first one who threatened her patient. She also thought about the young sailor who had jumped through gunfire, ready to subdue the smuggler captain.

If she'd followed her father's advice, she'd have been finishing medical school soon, Kathy thought. After that a surgical residency, then she could make up to a quarter million a year. Now she crouched next to a young corpsman paid a few hundred dollars a month, a woman determined, at the risk of her own life, to protect and heal her patient. Kathy swallowed hard.

Her father would never understand this, or her pride in

these people. You had to be here, to live things like this, to know what it meant.

"The chief will probably pull the bullet out when we get him back aboard ship, Ms. Shannon," Fiori said, bringing Kathy back to reality. "I've stopped the bleeding, cleaned the wound, and given him a shot for the pain. He's also had enough antibiotic to kill every germ on this ship."

"Good going, 'Doc'," Kathy said, patting the woman's shoulder. Bernadette Fiori smiled.

Kathy looked up. The captain's gig from *Lockwood* roared toward the freighter at high speed, filled with more armed men. Jeff Levine seemed to be with them.

"I'm going up to the bridge," she said to Goldhaver, "to see how the gunner made out."

"For Pete's sake be careful, Kathy. Don't get yourself shot," Goldhaver said weakly.

"You, Lieutenant, ought to take your own advice," she said, patting his cheek. He laughed.

Kathy pulled another clip out of her pistol belt, jammed it into the pocket of her trousers, and hurried toward the bridge ladder. The heavy flak jacket chafed her as she climbed the stairs.

"Gunner, how's it going up there?" she shouted to Apriliou, about forty feet away and twenty feet above her on the bridge. She wanted to be sure he knew who was climbing the ladder toward him.

"All secure, Ms. Shannon," the gruff voice answered. "Been a milk run since the shooting stopped."

She climbed the ladder to the bridge deck and looked into the pilothouse. Every window was shot out; two smugglers sat on the floor, arms clutched around their wounds. *Two more cases for Fiori.*

"You had good instincts about this, Ms. Shannon," Apriliou said. "We were ready for 'em after you had us lock and load." He looked at her as though he knew she hadn't seen men shot before, perhaps to distract her.

Kathy nodded.

When she walked down to the main deck, the other sailors held a half dozen freighter crewmen with hands over their heads.

A minute later, Lieutenant Commander Levine, a pistol in his hand, thick glasses and all, dashed across the quarterdeck, followed by six more armed sailors who fanned out and began to open the cargo hatches on the flat forward deck. The freighter's crewmen were facedown on the deck now, rifles pointed at their backs.

"What the devil happened here?" Levine said.

"A little communication problem," Kathy replied, "but we fixed it. Our Coast Guard friend needs a tire patch," she said, pointing to Goldhaver, who now stood unsteadily, his arm immobilized in a makeshift sling. "But 'Doc' Fiori seems to be keeping him amused for the moment."

"That Shannon gal is dangerous, XO," Goldhaver said.

"Well, Coastie, from what I can see, better that we have her on our side." Jeff Levine clasped his hand firmly around Kathy's shoulder. The politically correct rules about personal contact weren't meant for times like this, she thought.

"Good going, Kathy. Good work," Levine said.

"Thanks, XO. With all this shooting, these cats must have a hold full of dope."

"Let's have a look," Levine said. "Hold on a second." He raised his short-range radio.

"Delta India One, this is Delta India Two. Suspect ship has been confiscated, crew of eight under arrest, one drug crew fatality. Lieutenant Goldhaver has a treatable bullet wound being tended by 'Doc' Fiori. Recommend Lieutenant (jg) Shannon take command of the prize crew and run this bucket into Miami, Captain."

Kathy was astounded. Regulation and tradition both prescribed that the XO of the capturing ship take the prize in. Levine put his hand over the mouthpiece of the radio.

"No," the radio crackled, "either you take it in, XO, or we'll send a department head."

"Sorry, Captain, I'm not reading you. Say again, over."

Levine clamped his hand over the microphone and motioned to Kathy that he was going to move farther forward and talk to the skipper on the radio. The XO remained there three or four minutes, pacing back and forth, sometimes gesturing with his hands as he spoke.

"Who do you want for an engineer, Kathy?" he said when he returned.

"But I thought the skipper said he wanted you or one of the department heads . . . ?"

"He's . . . changed his mind."

"I don't know what you did, XO, but thanks. I'd like Roy Hobbs, Chief Varsik, and the chief's choice of engine room watchstanders. I'll need a little while to sort out the other stuff we'll need, and I'll have to get some clothes from the ship."

"Take your time. We'll finish up here."

Kathy thought about Levine's clandestine conversation with the CO. "XO, don't get in trouble over me on this one," she said.

"You pulled this whole thing off after Goldhaver got shot. Go for it, Kathy," he said.

"Hey, Commander Levine, take a look at this!" one of the sailors shouted from the forward hold. The man held up a plastic bag filled with white powder. "This sure ain't bread flour, and there's a load of it up here. Boxes and boxes—we're still counting 'em."

"Good going, Seaman Walsh," the XO shouted. "Keep counting."

"Quite a morning's work, Kathy," Levine said.

"Well, what needed doing was pretty clear," she replied.

Kathy turned to Jack Goldhaver. "Sir. You *have* placed all these people under arrest and confiscated this ship in the name of the United States government, right?"

"Right, Kathy. You're my witness."

One of the eight captured crewmen lying on the deck

with hands bound behind him looked up at her and cried out.

"¡Diabla perra!" he spat, his face contorted with hatred.

Instantly, the bilingual American sailor Juan Torres planted his booted foot firmly on the middle of the man's back. The muzzle of his rifle was jammed against the smuggler's neck.

The young sailor looked up at her.

"What he said was not very nice, Ms. Shannon."

"I got the message, Petty Officer Torres."

"Yes, ma'am. You would like perhaps that I teach this hombre some manners?"

"No, no," Kathy said softly. "He will have years in prison to learn his manners . . . many years. Please translate that for him exactly."

Torres nodded and smiled, speaking distinctly in Spanish as he prodded the base of the smuggler's skull with the cold muzzle of his rifle.

Chapter Nine

"Hey, Kathy," Goldhaver said as the corpsman led him toward the laddered stairway to the whaleboat, "you and 'Doc' saved my bacon today. I owe you both one."

"Come on, Lieutenant," Fiori said impatiently, tugging on the big man's good arm, "we've got to get you back aboard, maybe take that bullet out. You're wasting your strength with this talk."

"You only get to take the slug out if you give me a good belt of medicinal whiskey, 'Doc'."

Fiori rolled her eyes.

"I won't forget, Kathy," Goldhaver said, his face thoughtful now. "Or you either, 'Doc'."

Fiori smiled, then led him down the ladder and helped him into the pitching, rolling boat.

Kathy turned to examine her new, if temporary, command.

What a rustbucket, she thought. She had no idea of its seaworthiness or navigational equipment. Jeff Levine agreed to give her QM3 Thomas. Maybe she should ask for Gary McCloud, but the skipper probably wouldn't let his miracle-working electronics technician off the ship while deployed. On second thought, having McCloud around might be a bad idea.

How much grief would the exec take for pushing the prize crew captain's job for her with the CO? The old man wouldn't have done that on his own. But when she delivered this drug-laden ship to Drug Enforcement Administration agents in Miami, *Lockwood* and everyone aboard, including the skipper, would look good. She had to keep her word and bring the tired old ship safely to port.

Within an hour, she'd returned to the frigate, packed a bag, gathered up her crew, and seen the CO. She noticed Commander Taylor didn't keep her waiting this time.

"Lieutenant Shannon, are you sure you want this assignment? I'll put one of the department heads on, someone with more experience, if you're not comfortable with it."

Kathy shrugged, as though there were nothing to it. "Captain, this is the only command I'll have for a while. You've given me some of our best people. I won't let you down." Better to make Taylor feel as though *he'd* picked the prize crew.

As the captain's gig took the prize crew to the captured freighter, they passed the motor whaleboat coming back. The drug crew members were handcuffed and under armed guard. She saw a body bag laid out in the boat, and wondered if it was the man who had shot Jack Goldhaver, and the same smuggler she'd shot at. Kathy quickly turned away.

She had a ship to command. Nonetheless, she shuddered, even in the warm breeze. Shoot-'em-up police work hadn't entered her mind before her tour with the Coast Guard. But no one had said military life would be easy, either. The Navy hadn't earned respect among its countrymen for doing the easy jobs.

"This ship has some real problems," Roy Hobbs said softly. He'd walked up to the bridge where Kathy stood, a half hour after they'd left *Lockwood* behind and set course for Miami. The oil and dirt on his khaki uniform told her he'd taken a hard look at the engine room.

Chief Machinists Mate "Pappy" Varsik walked up soon afterward, equally soiled. A slender, balding man, Varsik's remaining hair was gray, although he was in his mid forties. "Well, Captain," the chief said, "your new command is like a '39 Ford with all original parts . . . interesting, but worn out."

A sudden thrill accompanied being addressed as captain. Varsik's tone of voice was not facetious. Kathy *was* the officer in command.

"Can we sail this ship as far as Miami?" she asked. "If so, we're home free. Once we deliver it alongside the pier, it becomes DEA's headache."

"The last crew figured they could sail to their rendez-vous point and back home," Varsik said. "We better hope that bilge pump doesn't fail. We're taking on water, maybe through the shaft alleys. The main bearing seals are prob-ably shot."

Chief Varsik and his men had figured out the engine room and had a head of steam up. Susan Thomas had plot-ted a course to Miami, and checked the ancient long-range navigation, or LORAN, equipment to confirm their position. The Coast Guard high-endurance cutter *Hamilton* would join them before sunset to provide an armed escort. Kathy welcomed that now, with several million dollars' worth of confiscated narcotics in the hold.

Two hours later, they steamed at eight knots, headed north northwest. Petty Officers Johnson and Apriliou, to-gether with Susan Thomas and a couple of others, would run the bridge for the day and a half run into port. The old steam plant wheezed and clanked like a jalopy without a muffler. The ship creaked and shuddered its way through each wave. Fortunately, Kathy thought, the weather fore-cast was good all the way to Miami.

"Roy, you got us up and going in record time," she said.

"Thank the chief for that. Good thing you picked Pappy Varsik to come along. I'm a gas turbine engineer. Old-timers like Pappy cut their teeth on steam plants."

"He probably knows all the chewing gum and baling wire tricks, too," she said.

Roy looked at her, and hesitated for a moment as though he planned to say something.

"Some neat places to see in Miami, Kathy. I'll show you around when we get there. Perhaps we can have dinner, even walk along the beach."

Roy's sudden interest surprised her.

"That would be nice. We should have time after we turn over this ship and before we go back to *Lockwood*, or join her in Mayport."

Roy smiled now.

"I better get that bilge pump working better, or we'll be passing water buckets over the side all night," he said, and clasped his hand lightly around her shoulder. The touch wasn't the same as his friendly pat a week ago. Nor was his look as benign.

Kathy spent the next hour walking and crawling through each space on the ship, to ensure she knew where everything was. The captain's cabin was a tiny, smoky-smelling cubicle near the pilothouse. She opened the porthole to air the place out, pulled grubby sheets from the small bed, and started to look for clean linen.

She was stripping the bed when Susan Thomas knocked on the door.

"Look what I found in their chart locker, Skipper," she said as she held up a coffee-stained navigational map of the Caribbean. "This may be where they were headed before you nailed them. Right here." Thomas pointed to a rendezvous point about one hundred miles off the Florida coast.

Kathy examined the map. The course line, which originated off South America, weaved through the Caribbean, avoiding shipping lanes and some areas where drug interdiction forces had been working. Perhaps *Lockwood* found them because the ship was operating in a new search area.

"Good work," Kathy said, "but this changes everything. We better tell the Coast Guard what you've found, but we can't do that over a clear radio frequency. Question is, *when* were the druggies going to link up at this position to make their drop?"

"Why don't I figure out the speed of advance they were using from the log, then project a time when the rendezvous was likely?" Thomas said. "Anyone waiting for them wouldn't want to hang around too long."

"Good idea. Go ahead and do that, Susan."

"Okay, Ms. Shannon, but what if the smugglers got a radio message off when we stopped them, or even after the shooting started?"

"Then no one will be within a hundred miles of that drop point you located. You're right; maybe they did. If not, though, the Coast Guard and the DEA may be able to close down part of their American drug connection."

Roy walked up, his face serious. "Do you want the good news or the bad news first?" he said.

"I don't have to act on good news," she said.

"Either there's a bad main bearing seal or cracked shell plating somewhere in the hull. It's leaking water in faster than the pumps can push it out. Otherwise, one of those weasels we captured opened a scuttle valve before you got the drop on them."

"How do you plan to handle it, Roy?"

"We either find the leak, borrow a P500 pump from the Coast Guard, or we'll all need water wings by midnight. The ship's bilge pump is half useless. We don't have time to pull it apart, and no replacement parts if we did. All I can do for now is find that scuttle valve or that hole, if there is one, and shut it or plug it. The chief's looking for something to repack the pump."

"I'll get on the radio with the Coast Guard, try to push

up our rendezvous with them, and tell them we need one P500. What do you think?''

''If we need more than that, check out our supply of shark repellent and life rafts.''

Hobbs started to walk away.

''Hey, Roy . . . what about the good news?'' she said.

''We have enough fuel to make Miami . . . if we don't sink first.'' He smiled.

Two hours later, Roy returned. His uniform was ruined now, his face and body covered with oil and dirt.

''I know more about this ship than I care to,'' he said tiredly.

''That sounds like a great understatement,'' Kathy replied.

''There's no scuttle valve. We have a hole in the bottom, a gap in the shell plating where some rivets have rusted out. I found water bubbling up when I got about halfway aft. The good news is that it won't take much to stop it.''

''What are you going to do?'' she said.

''The old battle damage control trick. Pull a mattress off a crew bunk and jam it in there, wedge it in place with a timber, then monitor the leak to keep the pumps ahead of it. That'll hold us until the Coast Guard can lend us a P500.''

''You look like the prime candidate to get that mattress in place,'' she said.

''Oh, joy. After that, I'm going to look for a shower and another mattress, a dry one,'' he replied. Despite his attempt at humor, Rob Hobbs looked close to exhaustion. He had solved the major threat to the ship, at least for now, she thought.

Two hours later, Petty Officer Thomas reported a radar contact approaching at high speed.

''Get a visual on him soon as you can,'' Kathy said. ''We need to know whether it's a friendly.''

"What if it isn't?" Thomas asked.

"You'll get more rifle practice than you ever had at boot camp."

Thirty minutes later, Thomas, peering intently through binoculars, announced, "It's okay, Ms. Shannon, it's the Coast Guard." A half hour later, a large white cutter with a broad red stripe at the bow came within range.

"Send them a flashing light. Tell them we don't want to use the radio, even the bridge-to-bridge. Mention the chart you found, and have them send a boat."

Lights blinked back from the cutter.

"They want to know who's in charge."

"Send 'Shannon, LTJG USN, Commanding.' "

The lights blinked back and forth again.

"They're sending a boat for you," Thomas said.

"No, they're sending a boat for *us*. Gather up your charts and calculations. If you hadn't found that chart, we wouldn't have anything to go on. If this works, it's your show. I want Lieutenant Hobbs to come along, too. Chief Varsik and the gunner can run it here for a while."

"You've landed a live one here, Lieutenant Shannon," the cutter's skipper said as he looked over the freighter's marked map in the ships operations center. "You may have found us a rattrap to spring."

"Petty Officer Thomas discovered the chart, figured out the timing. If you're talking about a trap, that means we're the cheese."

"Something like that. Here's what I suggest," the Coast Guard commander of the cutter said. "I'll send a top-secret flash message to Coast Guard Atlantic Area, Atlantic Fleet, and the Western Hemisphere Group, tell them we've put a dozen-man armed guard aboard your ship with a Spanish-speaker to play the smuggler crewman on your radio. You head for the marked rendezvous point, on the chance that the pickup ship or boat turns up."

"Where's the rest of our cover in case these drug people are heavily armed?" she asked.

"Task Force will have to keep its surface units out of radar range of your area to avoid scaring off the bad guys. If the drug people turn up, we'll be on scene as quickly as possible to assist and will call in air cover in the meantime. If the druggies don't turn up, some of my men get a few days good liberty in Miami. Either way, you have additional armed people to protect the evidence."

"We're it until the posse comes over the hill," Kathy said.

"Right. But everyone will be well armed for a shootout. If you have a better plan, let's talk about it."

"No, Captain, that sounds like the best we can do on short notice," she said. "We'll start looking for code names, or something like that, around the freighter, with the help of your Spanish-speaker. The drug people might have some exotic recognition drill for voice radio."

"Good idea. My Signalman Second Class Alvarado has done this before. He's sharp, can talk the birds out of the sky in Spanish, with a Colombian accent. Also a first-rate shooter when things get hot."

"We also need a P500 pump to nurse a hole in our hull and a tired bilge pump. We have no time to fix it and still make our rendezvous."

"You've got it, Skipper," the Coast Guard commander said, smiling at her.

"By the way, sir, please info USS *Lockwood* on your messages. My CO will be very unhappy if we get some action and I can only tell him about it later."

"He may envy you afterward."

"Maybe, maybe not," she said, and shrugged. Too late to worry about that now.

The dozen Coast Guardsmen who clambered aboard the *Marialena* carried weapons, clothing, ammunition, food, and radios. An amazing amount of gear, Kathy thought, for such a short voyage. The weapons included machine guns. They were expecting big trouble.

"Navigator, set a course for the rendezvous point," she said to Susan Thomas.

"Aye, aye, Captain," Thomas replied.

"Engine room, give me as much as you've got down there without blowing safeties on the steam plant," she said into a brass tube.

"What if that's not enough speed, Kathy . . . er, Captain?" Roy was still down there.

"Then, if you and Chief Varsik agree it won't leave us dead in the water, we tie down the safeties. We don't want to be late for the big party."

"Aye, aye . . . Captain," Roy said. "By the way, that mattress is holding. The pumps are gaining on the bilges."

"Good going, Roy. Let's make turns for twelve to thirteen knots. We're going to need that to make the rendezvous point by sunrise. Meanwhile, let the chief take over down there, and you check out the fresh water system. You've earned a hot shower, if there's any such thing."

A chunky, dark Coast Guardsman waited patiently for her to finish the conversation. When she turned, he saluted.

"Petty Officer Ramón Alvarado, Captain. I'm your translator and duty Latino when we talk to the drug scum out there."

"Your captain speaks highly of you."

"We've had a few successes, ma'am."

Alvarado's eyes went to the .45 on Kathy's hip.

"Been in combat before, Captain?"

"We had some live action down there this morning." She nodded toward the main deck.

Kathy still had a hard, burning spot in her stomach over the body bag going back on the gig.

Alvarado nodded.

"We'll change into civilian clothes to create cover, and hide our weapons along the main deck where they can't be seen. My men will find a place to sleep."

Another man stepped forward out of the growing darkness, saluted briefly, and reached out his hand.

"Lieutenant Ed Morse, Captain. Petty Officer Alvarado summed it up pretty well. We're the bait in the trap. Heaven only knows what kind of help we'll get, and how fast, if the bad guys come out for the goodies."

"There's enough cocaine in the hold to draw every rat for miles around," Kathy said. "Several million, minimum, from what I saw this afternoon. Perhaps some other stuff, too. We've been too busy staying afloat to do an inventory."

"Time enough for that in Miami," Morse said. "We fight, the bean-counters count. You say you have engineering trouble?"

"A hole in the hull and a tired bilge pump, but we have it under control."

"Good," he said. "Hate to win the battle and then have to swim home."

"Do you know a Lieutenant Jack Goldhaver?"

Morse smiled. "Jack the Hulk creamed me in enough intramural football scrimmages at New London that I'll probably hate him forever. But I'd sure like him around on a job like this."

"He was, this morning. Until he took a round."

"Bad?" Morse looked hard at her for the answer.

"Our corpsman kept him from bleeding out, and had him patched up and stabilized even before we sent him back to *Lockwood*. He'll be okay in a while."

"Heads-up stuff. Who's your corpsman? What's his name?"

"*Her* name is HM3 Bernadette Fiori. She had Goldhaver's pistol at the ready next to her while she bandaged him."

"Sounds like a tough lady."

"As tough as ninety-eight pounds gets," Kathy said.

"For sure then, we're all in this together."

Kathy Shannon grinned. "Was there ever any doubt?"

Chapter Ten

Kathy climbed down the steel ladder into the sweltering, steamy engine room at 10:30 P.M. Chief Varsik and his men had kept the *Marialena* moving forward at twelve knots despite the balky, rheumatic engineering plant. Puffs of vapor whistled occasionally from safety valves straining their limit. A young sailor watched the pressure gauges constantly.

A cardboard box of pipe patches and clamps lay in the corner. Another sailor, a boilerman, slept soundly on the steel deckplates amid the noise and heat, his work jacket beneath his head. An exhausted Roy Hobbs had left an hour earlier to steal a few hours' sleep.

"Chief, I'd like everyone armed down here," Kathy said. "Just in case we're boarded."

Varsik nodded. His frown said the prospect didn't please him.

"Mr. Hobbs will relieve me at midnight," he said. "When does the action start?"

"We'll reach the rendezvous point after first light. . . . Stand by for plenty of action if they're there. If the smugglers sent a radio message this morning when the shooting started, though, this whole drill is for nothing.''

On the *Lockwood*, Executive Officer Jeff Levine was working late. The duty radioman appeared with the outgoing message from the cutter *Hamilton* to the task force commander and Coast Guard Eastern Area proposing the trap scenario.

The XO groaned as he read about the old freighter and the risky proposal to lure the drug smugglers. Kathy *must* have agreed to the plan, he thought. But, after all, she was the prize crew captain, and had all authority to act. The old man wouldn't like this. He'd find a way to ruin her, Levine thought, if any of his sailors got shot up.

He initialed the message and handed back the clipboard. ''Take this to the skipper right away, please,'' he told the sailor.

Levine thought of Lieutenant Jack Goldhaver, who lay in his stateroom awaiting transfer to the stores ship *Sylvania* tomorrow. Chief Andrews and Bernadette Fiori had pulled out the small-caliber bullet that afternoon. Fiori's face, he'd heard, had turned gray during the operation. A larger slug might have shattered Goldhaver's shoulder bones, the chief said, or ricocheted into his vital organs.

Levine worried about how Kathy and *Lockwood*'s other people would fare tomorrow.

Kathy slept soundly until the knock on her cabin door at 0220. She swung out of the narrow, lumpy rack, then straightened out her wrinkled uniform.

Petty Officer Alvarado stepped into the room. Dim light poured into the darkened cubicle from the passageway behind him.

''The message is in, ma'am. Task Force says go for it. They coordinated with Coast Guard Miami, Western Hemisphere Group, and Atlantic Fleet.''

Kathy read the slip of paper, stamped out by a portable

printer the Coast Guardsmen had brought along. They were authorized to do anything necessary, from taking the drug dealers' calm surrender to a full-blown firefight. The list of commands and agencies on the classified message included every federal office engaged in the anti-drug effort.

"We'll close with them sometime after first light," she said, "depending on how much steam the engineers can keep up.

"One of our people is with your watch section on the bridge, monitoring the radar," Alvarado said. "With these civilian radar sets, the bad guys will know we're here about the time we spot them."

"If we're lucky, they won't suspect who we really are until it's too late," she said.

"Right, ma'am . . . if we're lucky."

"Could still be a trap, couldn't it?" Kathy asked.

"With the street value of what's down in the hold, Cap'n, it sure could," Alvarado said.

"Especially when the bad guys see no other surface forces on their radar scope," she said. "They could think we're steaming unescorted and don't know we're well armed."

"That's the game," the Coast Guardsman said.

"Okay. Be ready at first light, about 0515."

"Right, ma'am."

"Do you have any spare flak jackets? They sure saved a bunch of my people yesterday."

"Sure. You want one, Lieutenant?"

"I want my bridge watch to have them first. When this blows, they'll concentrate on shooting up our command and control."

"We have spares, Skipper. I'll make sure you have one, too. Good night."

Kathy kicked off her shoes and climbed back into bed. *What have I gotten us into*? she asked herself. Frightening thoughts of possible combat tomorrow raced through her mind. On the other hand, perhaps the threat of the heavily armed Coast Guard boarding party would force a surrender by the drug smugglers—if any of them were up ahead at all.

Her alarm clock beeped annoyingly at 0430. Kathy's muscles ached with tiredness and apprehension. The morning ahead might be a nightmare, but she must get up and face it. After she'd splashed water on her face and checked her pistol, she heard a knock on the door.

"Kathy, this is Roy. Okay to come in?"

"Sure," she said.

His eyes widened as he saw her standing there with a pistol in her hand.

"Nothing personal, you understand," she said.

He smiled. "Some sense of humor for this early in the morning."

"Better with some coffee." She yawned as she ran her hand through uncombed hair.

"You, Kathy Shannon, are something else," he said.

Roy's comment sounded more than comradely.

"Be careful out there today," he said.

"I will," she said as she slid a clip into the butt of the pistol.

"Just keep your head down, will you?"

"You be careful, too," she said. "I don't want anything to happen to my crew, either." She patted his shoulder. "Including my chief engineer."

She began to turn away.

"I meant what I said, Kathy," he said. "I don't want anything to happen to you." His voice had a sharper edge now.

"I know that, Roy," she replied softly. His words sounded personal, and concerned, she thought. ". . . and you wear your flak jacket, and keep it secured."

He smiled.

"Yes, Captain. I'll take that as an order," he said.

"After this is over," she said, "we'll enjoy Miami, and

you can show me that beach.'' *We'll have a great time, if we survive the next few hours,* she told herself.

Roy smiled again and nodded. As he departed, he closed the door quietly behind him.

Petty Officer Alvarado came by a few minutes later. The Coast Guardsman handed her another radio message.

"Satellite shot late yesterday confirms two fishing boats steaming near the area of our rendezvous," he said.

"Two?" That meant they would have tactical advantage. "How's the fishing there, generally?"

"Lousy, Captain. Miles from the usual fishing grounds."

"Where's Lieutenant Morse now?"

"Positioning our people, just in case."

"You mean for *when* we engage, don't you?"

Alvarado smiled.

"I promised you this," he said, passing her a flak jacket. "Your people on the bridge already have theirs."

She took the heavy, bulky vest. Difficult to move around in, but it could also save her life, she thought.

The cool breeze was stronger than Kathy remembered as she walked up the passageway and stepped into the *Marialena's* pilothouse. Perhaps she felt the chill more because all the windows had been shot out during the previous morning's unpleasantness.

"Air-conditioning works fine, Cap'n," Harry Johnson wisecracked. Her lanky first-class boatswain's mate from the *Lockwood* wore a pistol, and held a cup of coffee in his right hand. The men sleeping on either side of the pilothouse had rifles lying beside them.

"They needed the sleep more than we needed lookouts now," he said. "Our Coast Guard buddy is tracking the world on radar out there. Hey, McGrath," he said to the radarman, "can you pull up 'Good Morning, America' on that thing?"

"Sorry, Boats, all I see is 'Jeopardy,'" McGrath quipped.

McGrath had an ironic sense of humor.

"Do you have a flak jacket, Boats?" Kathy asked.

"Alvarado brought me one, Skipper. It's in the corner. I'll put it on when we get closer."

"Make sure *all* our watchstanders wear theirs once we get a visual on the targets. Two fishing boats up ahead could mean trouble. The Coast Guard people will play the decoys. We'll support them with fire, if need be."

"Yes, ma'am. . . . and thanks for the vest," he said.

Kathy stepped down the iron stairs into the hot, oily smelling engine room. Steam poured from every valve now. Connecting rods thrust up and down like the legs of a giant grasshopper. She watched a young sailor with a flashlight walk slowly through the engine room, painstakingly checking the hull and the valves.

"This is our version of Condition One," Roy said. "Only one watertight bulkhead with a door, forward below the main deck. It separates the cargo area from our engine spaces. Looks pretty solid. It's dogged down tight."

"Where are your weapons? Do you have enough ammunition?"

Roy nodded to his left. Service rifles stood stacked in the corner and bandoliers of ammunition sat piled on the deck.

"What do you think, Kathy?" he asked.

"Prepare for the worst. Two drug boats up ahead, not just one as we'd expected."

"We'll be ready to answer all bells, although I'd rather be up there with you when the shooting starts. Please keep your head down, will you? Remember what I said."

She looked at him.

"Please," he murmured.

"Okay, okay," she said impatiently, and turned to climb back up the ladder. Other parts of the ship needed inspection before dawn, but she wouldn't forget the warmth of Roy's smile.

* * *

"What's going on, Navigator?" Kathy asked Susan Thomas as she reached the top of the stairway to the *Marialena*'s bridge and peered into the dark pilothouse. The doors that led to the bridge wings outside were wide open. Boats Johnson paced from one side of the ship to the other, his binoculars scanning the horizon for the running lights of any surface contacts. Dim glows shone up from the compass and the radar set. The first hint of dawn appeared on the eastern horizon.

"Two small radar contacts, Cap'n, bearing three one zero degrees, thirty miles," the sailor monitoring the radar said.

She turned. Coast Guard Lieutenant Ed Morse stood in the dark corner. His grubby civilian disguise in preparation for the upcoming battle made him resemble the people she'd shot at yesterday morning.

"What do you think, Ed?" she said.

"They're not trawling this far out," he replied.

"What's your battle plan?"

"We'll take care of that. Just maneuver the ship to where we can either board or engage these people," Morse said. "We'll do the rest."

"Wait a minute," Kathy said. "When this fight is over, I write any next-of-kin letters. The Navy holds me responsible for everything that happens on this ship until I sign it over to DEA. We'll discuss your proposal in detail, and agree on a plan."

Morse's expression changed, and his body tensed. His look, she thought, reflected anger, frustration, or both.

"Okay, you're the captain," he said. "But we've done this drill before."

"Your drill, my ship, my people. Let's talk." Kathy nodded toward her tiny stateroom aft of the bridge. *I won't argue with him in front of the crew,* she silently vowed.

"Steady as you go, Boats," she said to Johnson, who stood at the wheel.

"Aye, aye, Cap'n," he replied. His eyes looked straight ahead into the night.

Johnson appeared to ignore the struggle between the officers ten feet away as though he were deaf, and steered the *Marialena* on the course Thomas had set hours before.

"What's your plan, Ed?" she said when they reached her small cabin. Her tone was conciliatory but firm. They had to settle this out, and quick.

"Size them up, get close enough, then tell them who we are and that they're under arrest. Show we have superior firepower. Then we call in help, board them. If they go hostile on us, we slug it out until the cavalry gets here."

"You're optimistic," Kathy said. "Consider that they have two boats to our one. They may have both tactical advantage *and* superior firepower. Our element of surprise will last only long enough for them to load their weapons. They won't surrender with odds of two against one."

"Their superiority is temporary," Morse replied. "By now, we have plenty of forces over the horizon."

"The drug crowd doesn't know that," she said. "We should wait for a superior force on station before anyone boards and captures these drug people. Our job, as I see it, is to keep them occupied long enough for our forces to get here. I won't risk any of my sailors for flashy heroics."

"I want to keep the drug crowd from destroying any additional evidence," Morse said, "and grab whoever's running this operation here. Might lead to prosecution of some heavy hitters on the beach if we can capture these guys and the evidence quickly. The FBI and DEA can take it from there."

"Some additional evidence isn't worth anyone's life," she said. "We'll have to play the unpredictables as they come."

Morse took a deep breath.

"When does Alvarado begin his game with the drug people on the radio?" she asked.

"He's searching the radio bands now with a scanner to

intercept any transmissions from them to us. He'll tune your transmitter to their frequency and talk to them in fluent Colombian Spanish. His father emigrated to the U.S. from Medellín. Alvarado is worth his weight in pearls. We call him the 'Pied Piper.' ''

''What if they don't buy his pitch?'' she said.

''They'll either fight or run. If they run, your ships, or ours, will intercept them. They've already had the schnitzel. They just don't know that yet.''

''What happens when we get into a firefight?''

''Then you back us up with as much small-arms fire as your people can put out.'' Morse pulled a small black radio out of his back pocket and handed it to her.

''Walkie-talkie?''

''Right. Two frequencies, powerful and clear at short range.''

''Is one of your people a corpsman?'' she said.

''No. We have only one 'doc' on *Hamilton* anyway.''

Kathy wished she'd brought Fiori along. Too late now. No one planned on this.

A knock on the door interrupted them. Thomas poked her head in. ''Contacts bear three one zero, twenty-seven miles, Cap'n,'' she said.

''Very well,'' Kathy replied. *Constant bearing, decreasing range. By now, they probably have us on radar.*

Alvarado was next to knock on the door.

''Lieutenant Morse, I have a radio signal that may be our target. A lot of Spanish asking about Maria.''

''This ship's registered name is *Marialena*, according to her documents,'' Kathy said. ''That could be the drug crowd.''

''Don't answer until we have a visual on them,'' Morse said. ''The less time they have to be suspicious, the better.'' Alvarado nodded agreement.

After Kathy and Morse finished their discussion, she walked out on deck, took a deep breath, and looked around.

Dawn was breaking to the east, slowly shedding a warm,

shimmering glow over the water as the ship scudded along in a light breeze. It couldn't look more peaceful, she thought, or be more deceptive. At least the sun would be in the enemy's eyes as they approached.

Men in civilian work clothes moved around the main deck below her in the semi-light. They concealed weapons and ammunition behind the steel shell plating that formed the outer hull of the ship.

An hour later, the sun was well above the horizon; the ship surged forward through blue-green seas and threw salt spray over the bow as the cool morning breeze began to warm.

Susan Thomas studied the horizon through binoculars.

"Masts bearing three one zero. Look like fishing booms. Must be them," Thomas said.

"That tracks with the radar bearing, range twelve miles," the Coast Guardsman on the radar set sang out.

"Go ahead and talk to them, Petty Officer Alvarado," Morse said, then turned to Kathy. "We didn't find any code words during our search of the ship, only ID cards with some of the crew names. Pretty sketchy, but Alvarado will try to work his deception off that."

"You're late, Maria," the voice from the other ship crackled in Spanish over the radio. "What gives? We've been waiting for hours."

"A big problem with the pumps," Alvarado replied. "We're taking water in the engine room, had to slow down."

"Where's Pedro? Tell him I want to talk to him."

"He's in the engine room working on the problem. Do you have any pump gasket material over there?"

"Tell Pedro to come up and talk to me."

"I'll tell him you want to speak to him. It may be a while before he can come up. Out."

Forty minutes later, the radio crackled again. The ships were now a half mile apart. As she'd agreed with Morse,

Kathy navigated the *Marialena* toward a position between the two fishing boats.

"Where is Pedro? Get him up here now so we can arrange the transfer. I want to talk to him now!" The voice sounded imperious, nervous.

"This is Ramón," Alvarado said in Spanish. "Pedro said to tell you he is working on the pump. If we don't fix it we'll have an engine room full of water in an hour or so. He wants me to arrange the transfer."

Alvarado looked toward the two officers and turned off the radio handset.

"They want to talk to the captain, the one you captured yesterday. I don't know how long I can hold them off before they get suspicious."

"Do what you can. Your story about the pumps and the engine room sounds very convincing, if I read your Spanish right," Morse said.

"Two more small radar contacts, lying to and stationary bearing two seven zero, twenty miles," the Coast Guard radarman cried out.

"Our guys?" Kathy asked.

"Maybe, maybe not," Morse answered.

"Alvarado, tell Task Force on our satellite radio that we have the two contacts at one mile or less and we're closing them," Morse said. "Have them acknowledge. They ought to be moving our way, pronto, to back us up."

The *Marialena* continued to steam slowly toward the two fishing boats, complete with net booms, which looked very much, Kathy thought, like innocent trawlers. One was an older, wooden-hulled craft. The newer, steel-hulled one was probably faster.

Coast Guardsmen in civilian clothes walked on *Marialena*'s decks to show an appearance of normalcy. Kathy felt tightness in her muscles, the return of the churning in her stomach that started during yesterday's shootout. She wondered if this was how John Paul Jones, Decatur, and Spruance felt before they went into battle.

Alvarado continued to talk to the fishing boats on the radio. The voice had told him to close the distance and still demanded to talk to Pedro.

"Better get the bullhorn, Alvarado," Morse said. "We're about to tell them that they're all under arrest."

They were about two hundred yards away when Kathy saw flashes of light from near the bridge of the steel-hulled fishing boat. For an instant, she thought it might be someone signaling, until the *braaack* of automatic weapons fire echoed across the water.

"Hit the deck!" she shouted, pulling the Coast Guard lieutenant toward her. They landed together on the latticed wood floor of the pilothouse. About that time, bullets thudded against the ship's shell plating in front of the bridge. A few came through the glassless windows and ricocheted with a singing whine off the back wall of the pilothouse where they'd been standing seconds before. Johnson had dived for cover, and for his M-14 rifle. Another burst of fire tore into the electrical wiring behind Kathy and sent sparks flying through the pilothouse.

"Commence firing!" Morse shouted to his men on the deck below. Instantly, rifle and machine gun fire poured in a deafening roar from a dozen positions on the lower deck.

Alvarado hunched down in the passageway, his satellite radio set beside him.

"Now, Alvarado!" Morse said.

"Task Force Command, this is *Red Duck One*. We are under attack, repeat, under attack. Automatic weapons fire incoming. Returning fire. Request immediate assistance. Acknowledge. Over."

"Roger, *Red Duck One*," the voice on the radio answered. "Help is on the way."

Kathy crawled toward the corner to grab a rifle. *They should have named us* Sitting Duck One, she thought humorlessly.

Gunfire roared from the main deck as Coast Guardsmen raked the sides and superstructures of the fishing boats. The thuds and pings of return fire against the freighter's hull sounded like hail now. The two fishing boats maneuvered to bracket the *Marialena* between them, forcing the freighter into their crossfire. Kathy's knees suddenly felt shaky, her breathing faster. *We have to break out of here before they tear us to pieces.*

"Ed, we're going to charge right down the middle," Kathy said, hoping there was no quaver in her voice. "We'll rake 'em with fire from both sides, and swing around. I'm going to ram the wooden-hulled one."

"Ram it? Are you crazy?" Morse replied.

"Two against one means we'll have to run from them till help arrives, however long that is. That steel hull is faster and more maneuverable than we are. If we attack, we improve our odds. Ramming one of them should make the druggies panic. They won't expect that."

"Okay, but if you bust a seam and take on water, we'll all be swimming. Your pumps aren't great right now."

"I'll take that chance. His wooden seams will crunch faster than our steel ones. Engine room, all ahead full!" Kathy said. "Tie down those safeties. Give me everything you've got!"

Susan Thomas jumped up from the deck, then emptied a clip of rifle fire at the ship off their starboard side before she ran in to take the wheel.

"I've got it, Boats," Thomas shouted. Johnson grabbed his rifle and helped Gunner Apriliou rake the bridge area of the other fishing boat with fire.

The *Marialena* lurched forward as Roy and Chief Varsik opened the steam valves down below.

"Left full rudder," Kathy ordered. "Come about and draw a bead on that wooden hull, Susan. We're going to ram them."

"Ram 'em? Hot dog! Let's go git 'em." the younger woman said as she put the wheel over sharply. "Rudder is left full, Cap'n." The large helmet and flak jacket made the dark, slender Thomas look chunky.

Johnson turned to look for more ammunition. Kathy tossed him a bandolier, which he shared with Apriliou. The range was opening now, and firing stopped temporarily.

"Wow!" the radarman shouted, returned now from outside where he fired at the steel-hulled boat on the starboard side. He peered intently into the radar scope. "I've never seen faster surface contacts! Those two at twenty miles a few minutes ago are now at twelve. They must be closing at forty knots or better!"

"Must be Pegasus-class Navy hydrofoils from Key West," Kathy said to Morse.

"Yeah, we could use their three-inch guns right now."

"Might want to tell the men up forward what we're going to do," she said.

"I'm going down there." Morse stepped out on the bridge wing. "We're going to ram the wooden hull," he shouted to the men below. "We'll reopen fire when we get back in range to keep them pinned down. Hold off till I give the word. Take cover . . . and hold fast when we're about to ram. The impact will shake your teeth loose." Then Morse clambered down the steps to join his people.

As the freighter came about in a wide circle to port, men below frantically opened ammunition crates and reloaded weapons. Brass shell casings littered the deck from the last skirmish.

"Engine room, we're maneuvering to ram one of the fishing boats," Kathy shouted down the voice tube. "Give me everything you've got. Be prepared to evacuate fast if we bust a seam." There was nowhere to go if they did. The life rafts were probably full of holes by now.

"Roger, give 'em hell, Kathy," Roy replied.

He probably didn't like being below decks with all the action up here, Kathy thought.

"Start leading that wooden hull, Susan," Kathy shouted.

"You mean like leading ducks with a shotgun, Skipper?" Thomas asked.

"Exactly. Once he figures out what we're doing, he'll

change course in a hurry. Be careful. They'll try to concentrate fire on our bridge again.''

Suddenly a thundering roar swept over the ship. When Kathy looked up, two Navy F-14 Tomcat fighters streaked over the water at fifty feet, made a wide turn, and headed back toward the two fishing boats.

''He's changing course again, Lieutenant!'' Thomas shouted.

The wooden-hulled fishing boat moved slowly across their bow several hundred yards ahead.

''Engine room, is that all you've got?''

''You want maybe I should get out and push?'' Roy shouted back up the tube.

The fishing boat had reacted too late, Kathy thought. Frantic Spanish, including what sounded like colorful profanity, rang out over the smuggler's radio.

''I think you have their attention, Lieutenant,'' Alvarado shouted from the passageway. ''I don't know whether they're more angry, or more scared.''

''Give 'em something else to think about. You might tell them they're under arrest, and their boats are now the impounded property of the United States government,'' she shouted back.

Alvarado grinned, and cranked up the radio again.

As the range closed, Kathy saw flashes of gunfire erupt again from the wooden fishing craft.

''Commence firing,'' Morse roared from the main deck.

A fusillade of bullets cut a stitchwork of holes and splintered wood across the bridge of the wooden fishing boat.

''What I couldn't do with five more knots,'' Thomas muttered with exasperation, her hands tight now around the wheel, her foot drumming nervously on the deck.

The fishing boat suddenly slowed. Perhaps the gunfire had cut a vital control or taken out their helmsman.

''Pour it into 'em!'' Morse roared. Gunfire erupted again from the deck below.

The smugglers were at a disadvantage, Kathy thought.

The *Marialena* showed them only a narrow head-on profile, while the entire side of the drug vessel was exposed.

"All hands, stand by to ram!" Kathy shouted into the voice tube to the engine room. Morse cried out the same message to the men on the main deck.

A man burst out the bridge door of the fishing boat and fired a machine gun toward them as the two vessels rapidly closed each other. Bullets ricocheted off the bridge plating near them. Seconds later, he lurched, pitching headlong down the ladder to the deck.

"Won't be a clean hit, Ms. Shannon," Thomas said.

"Nail 'em however you can," Kathy replied. She saw every detail of the boat now, including the frightened, cursing faces of crew members on the deck. Firing continued.

Suddenly, Kathy felt like she'd been slammed in the chest with a sledgehammer. She spun around and landed facedown on the deck, unable to catch her breath. *I'm hit.*

In seconds, Johnson's strong arms had rolled her over. Through the blur of her sudden shock, Kathy saw him up there, saying something to Thomas and Apriliou. Suddenly, his rough hands slapped her lightly across the face.

As she came out of semiconsciousness, she heard him say, "She's okay, she's okay. The vest stopped the round. Just knocked the wind out of her."

Kathy felt the jarring crunch as Thomas steered the *Marialena*'s bow midships into the port side of the fleeing fishing boat. The freighter stopped dead. Everyone struggled to stay on their feet, and grabbed anything to hold onto.

"Help me up, Boats," Kathy said when the ship stopped, still groggy but starting to come out of shock.

She stood in time to see the freighter's steel bow jammed into the fishing boat like a knife in a block of cheese. The loud crunching and snapping of disintegrating wood that accompanied the shocking jar had sounded like fireworks.

"All engines stop," Kathy started to call out. The words came out a weak croak.

Johnson leaned over the voice tube. "All engines stop!" he shouted into it.

Men on the main deck raised their guns again and fired into the wounded drug boat.

"All back full," Kathy said. Boats again called the order into the tube. In seconds, a great gush of water came from the stern, and a shuddering lurch backward pulled the old freighter out of the fishing boat like a dagger from a wound. The wooden craft broke in two and began to sink, its net booms cocked now at a crazy angle as it listed to port.

"Alvarado . . . get on the bullhorn," Morse shouted. "Tell them to surrender now or we'll let the sharks have them for lunch."

The young Coast Guardsman's voice boomed out instantly in clear Spanish. Men appeared on deck, hands in the air. They ran to the side of the dying boat and plunged into the water.

Suddenly a cold rush shot up Kathy's back. She was recovering quickly now.

"Boats, quick, where's that other fishing boat, the steel hull?" she snapped. *I screwed up. Should have watched the other boat, too.*

"He's heading west like the devil's on his tail, Ms. Shannon. They know the game's up. They're trying to make a run for it."

Kathy let her breath out slowly and began to relax. The hydrofoils would intercept the other drug boat. Perspiration soaked her face and underarms now.

"Thanks, everybody. For a minute, I thought I'd bought the farm. Good, quick diagnosis, Boats. Petty Officer Thomas, come about to port; maneuver to pick up survivors. Have the engine room give us bare steerageway."

"Maneuvering to pick up survivors, aye . . . Captain," Thomas responded, her face in a broad smile now.

Armed Coast Guardsmen rushed to the accommodation ladder and pulled sputtering, fearful men from the water, frisked them hurriedly, forced them facedown on the deck, and snapped plastic handcuff strips around hands clasped behind their backs.

Sharks, Kathy thought. *Good thing I didn't think of them before.* She shuddered. The larger pieces of the fishing boat began to disappear beneath the surface. Flotsam drifted everywhere. The remaining drug crewmen swam frantically toward the *Marialena*'s ladder.

Naval gunfire behind them made Kathy and Morse look off their stern. Two gray hydrofoils with Navy markings, riding high above the water, converged on the remaining drug boat. The noise had been a warning burst from their three-inch guns across its bow, she thought.

"We won't have to ram *that* one." Morse chuckled as he climbed up the ladder to the bridge.

"We didn't do badly," she said.

"Close call, eh?" Morse said, tapping the front of Kathy's flak jacket where the bullet had torn the covering where it hit, close to her heart. "You were pretty darn lucky, lady."

She looked down. Without the flak jacket, she'd be dead now. Kathy felt a tingling weakness, almost a faint.

"I'll check for hull damage forward, Kathy." Roy's voice echoed up the voice tube from below.

"Roger," she said.

Alvarado walked out from the radio room, a broad smile on his face.

"We must be living right, Lieutenant," he said.

"What do you mean?" Kathy asked. *I'm lucky to be living at all.*

"Task Force has ordered us to make port in Key West with the hydrofoils as escort, instead of going into Miami. The Navy has no tanker nearby, and the 'foils will be in low-fuel state when they get back, after roaring out here at top speed to help us. Tough duty—a few days in Key West."

Right now, Kathy thought, she'd trade all this excitement

and success for a good night's sleep. She shuddered, although the breeze didn't feel chilly.

She raised her binoculars and saw the two hydrofoils with guns trained on the other fishing boat, which had now stopped. The radio squawked a warning in Spanish for everyone on the drug boat to raise their hands. So much for the drug boss who tried to run for it, she thought. Another earsplitting low pass by the F-14s over the fishing boat underlined the futility of escape.

"Kathy, remind me never to let you get angry at me."

She recognized Roy's voice. He looked out over the wreckage of the fishing boat, at the soaked crewmen now facedown on the *Marialena*'s deck. The front half of the wooden hull was about to sink. He walked over to her.

"You're okay up forward," he said. "No leaks, just a dent or two. It's all downhill from here . . . I think."

Then Roy's eyes went to the torn flak jacket cover. His eyes widened. He stepped toward her as though he would put his arms around her, then stopped.

"So that's why it wasn't your voice when we . . ."

Roy's hands tightened and loosened. He seemed unable to do anything useful with his arms now.

"I'm glad you're safe, Kathy. You took some big chances today. They should give you a medal and a half for this one."

"We'd never have done it without you," she said.

He smiled. ". . . and Chief Varsik, and his guys. Let's not forget them." His eyes told that he had other things to say. This wasn't the time. "We deserve a good time in Key West," he said, ". . . and I'll make sure you have one."

Chapter Eleven

An hour after the collision Kathy toured the ship with Roy. They peered over the side near the bow. Crumpled metal marked the point where the freighter had struck the fishing boat.

"Be glad you don't have to pay for this fender-bender, Kathy. We mashed a peak tank, but you have no leaks up here. Smart gamble, lady."

Roy turned to smile at her. "Looks like this ship's been through a demolition derby," he said. "We should run a contest to guess the number of bullet holes and dents . . . like those 'how many jelly beans in the jar' gimmicks."

Roy's easygoing nature had returned, she thought, once they'd secured the prisoners and set a course for Key West.

"Right. You think anyone will notice a crunched bow among all the battle damage?" She shrugged.

The two hydrofoils steamed a few hundred yards away at eight knots. That speed, she'd computed, would place the three vessels and the captured fishing boat near Key West in the early-morning hours of the next day.

Ed Morse had departed to board the steel-hulled fishing

boat and take it in. He left men behind to guard the prisoners. "You should consider a transfer to the Coast Guard, Kathy," he'd said before he left, taking her hand. "You have a talent for this kind of work, and a lot of guts. I look forward to seeing you in Key West."

Kathy had thought about Morse's words as he walked away. An inter-service transfer might get her a small command earlier, but she wanted a missile frigate like *Lockwood*. Later, if she made captain, she might land one of those big Aegis cruisers, or whatever held first place in the Navy surface ship inventory by then.

"How about some breakfast, Kathy?" Roy asked, interrupting her reverie. "Petty Officers Thomas and Briggs said they'd whip up hot food for everyone back in the galley. Briggs says he knew that experience at McDonald's would come in handy one day."

"Sure, Roy, good idea," she said. Now that the excitement was over, she suddenly felt exhausted. She suppressed thoughts of what would have happened without her flak jacket.

As she stretched out on the thin, lumpy mattress in the tiny captain's stateroom an hour later, Kathy wondered about the two men she'd dealt with in recent days.

She'd been surprised that Ed Morse had treated her so warmly before leaving, especially after their argument about tactics. He'd exposed himself to fire during the shootout as he darted from place to place to encourage his men. Ed showed himself accustomed to taking charge. He could also be charming. If he decided to follow up once they arrived in Key West, she'd be interested to learn more about him. He certainly knew by now that she spoke her mind and was one person he couldn't take charge of.

Roy had also been impressive. His success with the balky engineering system, and his fast response during the gun battle, kept the ship from being helpless amid deadly fire. He was lower-key than Morse, but reliable in a showdown. Roy also seemed attracted to her, she thought as she drifted off to sleep. No longer, either, did she regard him in the brotherly way that she had aboard ship before all this. The intervening crisis, she thought, had drawn them closer together.

Four hours later, still tired, Kathy walked slowly forward and took over the bridge to give her small group of watchstanders a break. No one had had much rest the last couple of days. Everyone had been exhausted by the deadly stress of the firefight. Susan Thomas had the helm. Thomas had been going nonstop since early morning, too. At least, Kathy thought, everything would be uneventful during the voyage into Key West.

At 2:34 P.M. a loud bang shook the ship. Oily black smoke gushed from the large ventilator pipe behind the bridge that served the ship's engineering spaces. Seconds later, Roy's voice shouted up through the voice tube.

"Fire! Fire in the engine room! Briggs is injured. I'm getting him out of here. Get CO2 extinguishers down here, quick." Roy was coughing as he spoke. A wisp of smoke filtered up the tube.

Kathy turned to Petty Officer Thomas. "I'll take the helm. Get Varsik and Alvarado to take extinguishers down there. Help Briggs when Mr. Hobbs brings him out."

Kathy seized the UHF radio microphone in one hand, the helm in the other.

"*Pegasus* and *Taurus*, this is *Red Duck One,*" Kathy said. "Mayday, Mayday. We have an engine room fire. Request you close *Red Duck One* and prepare to render firefighting assistance, over."

"*Red Duck One,* this is *Pegasus,*" the radio instantly crackled and barked. "We are changing course to close your port side with firefighting gear. Out."

"*Red Duck One,* this is *Taurus*. We will approach your starboard side. Out."

When Kathy glanced out the smashed pilothouse windows seconds later, *Pegasus* had already turned toward them. Across the water, she heard the continuous bonging sound of General Quarters alarms on both hydrofoils and saw men scurry about the decks. Oily smoke billowed from the ventilator now. *Marialena* lost speed and drifted toward a stop.

She rushed to the wing of the bridge and looked aft in time to see a smoke-blackened Roy, the unconscious Briggs over his shoulder, stagger from the engine room access door on the main deck. More smoke poured out the open entrance behind him. He handed the man over to two seamen and dashed back inside, his face now covered with a handkerchief. Thomas arrived seconds later with a first aid kit, then took Briggs aside and sat him down.

The two Coast Guardsmen watching the captured smugglers on the main deck looked up nervously at Kathy. "Stay where you are, and watch those prisoners *extra* carefully," she ordered.

The men unlimbered their rifles and pointed them toward the now-restless captives.

Seconds later, Varsik and Alvarado, each with a CO2 extinguisher, ducked through the doorway to the engine room. More smoke poured out as they opened the door, which they pulled shut behind them to keep drafts from fanning the flames.

Pegasus was almost alongside now. "We need men with CO2 extinguishers and OBAs ASAP," Kathy shouted into the radio microphone.

Oxygen breathing apparatus, or OBA, was equipment *Marialena* didn't have. It would keep rescuers from being overcome in the dense smoke. Sailors on *Marialena*'s deck caught lines from the hydrofoil and made it fast to the freighter.

Muffled shouts echoed from the engine room communication tube.

"Busted oil line . . . secure that fuel valve!" someone shouted.

Two *Pegasus* sailors holding extinguishers and OBAs clambered onto the freighter's deck. The ships were now firmly bound by lines to each other. The *Pegasus* CO, she thought, risked damage to his own ship if an explosion occurred.

Kathy thought of going down to the engine room herself, then stopped. There were too many people there already. She'd only be in the way.

Minutes stretched like hours. More garbled noises filtered up the voice tube. The other hydrofoil, Taurus, stood near *Marialena*'s starboard side. Some sailors poised on the deck with fire hoses and a foam generator, others with extinguishers and OBAs. The radio confirmed they were ready to board if needed.

The door to the engineering spaces clattered open again seconds later. Smoke poured out, but less this time. A *Pegasus* sailor with an OBA helped Roy out on deck. Alvarado followed. A second masked seaman held Varsik. Roy went to the side, grabbed the lifelines, and threw his head back, inhaling deeply. He coughed and spat over the side, then rubbed a sleeve of his uniform shirt across his blackened face.

As Kathy dashed down the ladder from the bridge toward Roy and the others, another sailor jumped over from *Pegasus* with a medical bag and headed for the men just helped out of the engine room.

"Are you all right, Roy?" she asked.

"Sure," he replied, coughed, spat again, and shook his head. "Just need a few minutes to get my breath back."

He looked like he'd been covered with oil, then rolled in soot.

"You were darn lucky, Mr. Hobbs," Varsik said, breathing heavily. "When the flames trapped you in the corner, I thought you were a goner."

No wonder Roy looked so singed. "What happened?" Kathy said.

"Fuel line ruptured, pumped oil all over. Fire started. Most of the oil ended up in the bilges, but continued to burn. The smoke overcame Briggs."

Roy paused and took another deep breath of fresh air.

"Tough part was shutting down the fuel supply feeding the fire. The old valve was stiff, hard to close. That engine room's a mess."

A tall, lean lieutenant in short-sleeved khakis jumped across between the ships and came up to her. Must be the CO of *Pegasus,* she thought.

"Looks like you have things under control here, Skipper," he said.

"I appreciate the fast work by you and your people. I'm Kathy Shannon." She held out her hand.

"Looks like you moved pretty smartly yourselves. I'm 'Duke' Philips," he replied.

"Roy Hobbs," Roy said. He held up a grimy hand rather than shake. "Sure appreciate the help. We ran out of everything down there at once, including time."

The corpsman had a stethoscope on Varsik's chest as Alvarado waited his turn. Neither had been below as long as Roy, Kathy thought.

"Will you need a tow into Key West?" Philips asked.

Kathy turned to Roy Hobbs. Before he could answer, she heard Varsik's husky voice behind her.

"If we can cumshaw some damage control pipe patches and clamps, Skipper," he said to Kathy, "I'll get this bucket under way on her own power. The P-500 will clean out the bilges, then we'll ventilate the spaces to clear the smoke. A working party can clean up the engine room while we're under way."

"Sounds good to me," Roy said. "What do you think, Kathy?"

"First," she said, "let's make sure you three and Briggs are okay."

The corpsman nodded to her reassuringly and held his thumb up when she glanced at him.

"Roy," Duke Philips said, "why don't you and the other men come have a hot shower and a cold drink? We'll send a message up the chain about the fire."

When Roy returned forty-five minutes later, he looked revived. Varsik walked toward the engine room with a cardboard box full of parts to patch the pipe. They'd try to light the plant off in about an hour when he finished, Kathy thought.

"The chief was adamant about not being towed," she said.

"He told me over on *Pegasus* that no one was about to tow his ship while he was the leading machinists mate."

"Tough old bird," she said.

"That's why he's good."

"You're pretty tough yourself, Roy," she said.

"Just an old country boy, Kathy. Not smart enough to know when to quit."

"Sure, Roy . . . sure." She smiled.

Two hours later, with patches clamped around the ruptured fuel pipe, Roy and Chief Varsik cajoled the old engine back to life. *Marialena* was soon under way, limping along slowly, for her appointment with the Drug Enforcement Administration in Key West.

Chapter Twelve

Warm, humid breezes blew across the bow of the old freighter as Kathy stood on the starboard wing of the bridge. Coast Guard sailors on the pier stood ready to tend the lines. Slowly, she brought *Marialena* alongside the former Naval Station dock at Key West, Florida.

Even at eight in the morning, perspiration rolled off the brows of linehandlers, the heat mitigated only by a light breeze. Modernistic white condos faced the water in front of President Harry Truman's wooden summer White House of fifty years earlier.

The old engines shuddered as Kathy maneuvered the ship alongside the World War II vintage dock. Roy and the chief were both below to ensure that the engineering part of their landfall went smoothly.

At precisely 8:00 A.M., after the linehandlers finished doubling up the mooring lines, Susan Thomas snapped the American flag to the top of the old coastal freighter's stern truck. Boats Johnson, his boatswain's pipe in hand, sounded the piercing notes of ''Attention to Colors.'' The small U.S. Navy contingent faced aft and saluted.

85

I wish Dad could understand this, she thought, *the great people, the risk, why it's my destiny and my passion to do this, as his was to be a surgeon.*

Several hundred yards ahead, a white Dutch cruise liner occupied Mallory Dock. Expensively dressed tourists in casual clothes tripped easily down the brow of the luxury ship, ready for carefree fun in the United States' southernmost city.

She saw several civilians on the pier, Navy and Coast Guard officers, police cars and government sedans, and a dark bus with metal mesh over the windows. A prisoner van for her captives, she thought.

While the ship was secured, Roy came up to the bridge.

"Your first time in Key West, Kathy?"

"Yes, I'm looking forward to it."

"Terrific town," he said. "Great restaurants and lots to see. Looks like serious business out there first, though." He nodded toward the pier.

"Once they sign a receipt, this ship is theirs. A three-day command is probably some kind of naval record," she said.

"Add a firefight, a ramming, and an engine room fire, and I'm sure it is." He chuckled. "You don't need any more close calls like that last one, Kathy." His voice turned serious.

She didn't want to tell him about the bruise, still sore, where the bullet had struck the flak jacket.

"You had your own dicey moments, Roy. This was no picnic for you either," she replied.

Susan Thomas had left to go down to the main deck. For a moment, they were there alone. Roy took her hand. His grip was strong, but gentle.

"Let's go see Key West today, have a fun time. What do you say?" he asked.

"Okay, Roy," she said. When she glanced toward him, that look was in his eyes again. The touch of his hand was comforting, nice, she thought. Something told her they wouldn't simply be shipmates again after this.

"I'd better see to our welcoming party," she said reluctantly, "and get the day's business behind us. Meanwhile, work out something with Boats and the chief to get most of our people some liberty as soon as possible."

Kathy stood near the brow of the *Marialena,* ready to welcome the group aboard.

"Who's in command here, Lieutenant?" the civilian said as he walked aboard and displayed a badge and federal credentials.

"I am," she said. "My name's Kathy Shannon." She extended her hand.

"Ed Hayes, Drug Enforcement Administration, Miami. This is Special Agent Art Halloran of the FBI. We need to talk for a few minutes." Hayes did not introduce the other two men, both young, fit, and wearing dark sunglasses.

"Yes," she said, "but I want some other people there, too." She gestured toward the Navy and Coast Guard officers standing behind the civilians on the gangway.

"The crew's mess is the only place to sit down," she said to Hayes. She led them aft on the main deck and pulled open a door. "The narcotics you're looking for are in the forward two cargo holds," she said. The DEA man turned to the two behind him.

"Get Chico, and go have a look," Hayes ordered.

"Who are the other two?" she asked.

"Maritime Administration," he replied dryly, as though the answer were none of her business.

She doubted that, but decided not to pursue it.

For an hour, she and Roy described every aspect of the last day and a half. Alvarado detailed his radio conversation with the thugs. Susan Thomas told with enthusiasm how she'd sunk the wooden fishing boat on Kathy's order.

"Why did you ram the fishing boat?" Hayes asked, his

voice irritated. "We'd have additional evidence against this
crowd if you'd brought it in."

Roy began to speak. Kathy interrupted him, her eyes
flashing.

"First of all, we were alone, taking heavy automatic
weapons fire. Ramming was my best way to stop them. All
the evidence you need to put these people away is in the
forward hold, and on the second boat."

"Okay, okay. I didn't mean to second-guess you, Lieutenant." Hayes raised his hands, evidently surprised by
Kathy's reaction. "You all did a great job out there. You
had the right to call it the way you saw it."

"Right. My people did themselves proud," she replied.
"Our job included bringing them all home alive."

"We'd like to take the prisoners off," Hayes said, "go
through the ship for evidence, and interview some of your
crew, if that's all right with you, Skipper."

"We'll cooperate fully," Kathy said. "I want to get my
people ashore to unwind as soon as you've finished talking
to them. They've had a rough couple of days. I'll also sign
this vessel over to you, whenever you're ready."

One of the men with sunglasses came in, took Hayes and
Halloran aside for a minute, then left.

"You grabbed a big one," the DEA man said. "Well
up in the millions. There's so much, it'll take a while to
figure out its street value. When do you want to talk to the
press in Miami?"

"I don't," Kathy said.

"This is a *very* big drug haul," Halloran said slowly,
seemingly surprised. "Surely the Navy, and the Coast
Guard, too, deserves credit for making it happen."

"I'm a destroyer officer," Kathy replied. "I'd prefer to
keep it that way. I want to get back to my ship. Talk to
Washington, or Atlantic Fleet headquarters in Norfolk.
They'll provide a spokesperson for you."

"Okay, we can work that out later," Hayes replied, "but
the press likes first-person stories. Meanwhile, we'll unload

the drugs, book the prisoners, and examine the ship for evidence.''

''Petty Officer Thomas will give you the map they used that led us to the rendezvous point. By the way, somebody better patch the hole in the shell plating and fix the bilge pump,'' Kathy said.

The FBI and DEA agents stared at her blankly. Land-lubbers, she thought. They didn't have the faintest idea of what she was talking about.

An hour later, at 10:00 A.M., after debriefing with the Navy and Coast Guard officers, Kathy and Roy walked off the ship in casual civilian clothes into the warmth of the sunny morning. Most of the crew was already gone. Petty Officer Alvarado had promised to show Susan the town, and Kathy looked forward to Roy's tour of the famous city.

''Step over here, Kathy, so I can get you and your ship in the picture,'' Roy said, unlimbering his camera. ''This is one snapshot you'll want to show to your grandchildren.''

Kathy had a receipt from Agent Hayes assuming DEA responsibility for the vessel. She'd written on it that the ship needed immediate hull repair, and explained to him what it meant. No sense having the old *Marialena* settle by the pier.

Chief Varsik and Boats Johnson, who'd been to Key West often over the years, agreed to watch the ship. They wanted to go over for a cold beer or two later in the day. DEA had the Key West police seal off the pier.

The Coast Guard station across the inlet would berth *Marialena* after one of their cutters put to sea in a couple of days. She and Roy would move to the Navy bachelor officers quarters overlooking the yacht basin, and the crew would live on the Coast Guard base. They were on their own until *Lockwood* returned to Mayport a week later.

Kathy turned around once she was on the pier, and looked back at the *Marialena*. Even though she'd examined damage throughout the ship yesterday, the sight still made her shudder. Hundreds of bullet dents punctuated the hull and superstructure, had torn off paint, splintered wood, shattered glass portholes, and punched holes in doors.

A miracle, she thought, that no one on the *Marialena* had been killed, and that they'd made port safely after the engine room fire. Kathy said a silent prayer of thanks. Then she turned and walked with Roy toward Duval Street, the main thoroughfare of old Key West, five minutes away.

"Nice to be 'on the beach,' isn't it, Kathy?"

"Sure is. Beats having people shooting at you."

". . . and fuel lines rupturing in mid-ocean. Let's forget that and just enjoy our day."

He took her hand, lightly but firmly. The grip that linked them felt natural, comforting, she thought, as though it would be abnormal not to be holding his hand now.

"Europeans come to Key West by the busload to see the sunset on Mallory Dock," Roy said as they walked along. "Lots of neat old houses have become classy B&Bs. Nice beaches, skin diving, good food, you name it. This would be a terrific place for a honeymoon."

"I'll file that away for the distant future," she said. "I haven't even started looking for a fiancé."

Roy smiled.

"Anyway," he said, "I'll show you around. We can wind up with the sunset at Mallory Dock, after a draft beer at Sloppy Joe's on Duval and a nice lunch. I can even get you a cigar with tobacco grown from Cuban seed at a place on a side street here, if you like."

Roy laughed at her grimace. "Okay, you don't have to smoke the cigar. How about an ice cream instead?"

"I'll take the ice cream," she said, and squeezed his hand.

When Kathy turned in that night, she couldn't sleep right away. She pictured Roy, the self-proclaimed country boy from Milledgeville, Georgia. He'd shown no interest before, except friendly concern after *Lockwood*'s captain landed on her about the refueling. She hadn't thought of Roy as attractive, and knew little about him as a person before this. A male companion on the ship was the last complication she needed. Much had happened since they'd left *Lockwood* to change her mind. Roy was determined, thoughtful, and brave, qualities she couldn't ignore. He was also, she'd learned, tenderly demonstrative.

Kathy and Roy walked over to Mallory Dock a half hour before sunset. The cruise ship had loaded its tourists and departed hours before. People stood shoulder to shoulder and sat on the concrete rim. Skirling bagpipes belted out the Marine Corps hymn at the southern end. Hundreds faced west toward the fireball of the setting sun, took pictures, made small talk. Before them, a chunky man balanced a grocery cart full of bowling balls on his chin. Another man's trained cats leaped through flaming hoops, while a third performer towered above the crowd on a steel wire, making wisecracks to the crowd as he did somersaults.

"What do you think, Kathy?" Roy asked, drawing her lightly toward him as they walked along.

"Fantastic," she replied, and squeezed his hand again before she realized it.

The day, she thought, had been a dream. They'd walked the length of historic Duval Street, stood on the southernmost point in the United States, ninety miles from Cuba, and had their picture taken together. After that, they ate lunch at a neighborhood Cuban restaurant on a tree-covered, unpaved street off Truman Avenue. They were the only *Yanquis,* and second servings of black beans and rice came with the nod of the head.

They'd sauntered through Fast Buck Freddie's, a sophisticated Duval Street department store which she thought belied its name. Later there was Jimmy Buffett's restaurant and shop, and cold draft beer at Sloppy Joe's bar, a wide-open, rough kind of place with blaring rock music on lower

Duval that Ernest Hemingway had haunted forty years before.

As they'd strolled down a side street in the growing darkness en route back to the ship and Mallory Dock, Roy had spun her gently around to face him.

"It's been a wonderful day, Kathy, and it's not over yet." His kiss wasn't entirely unexpected, but it was on a public street, albeit in the darkness and under a palm tree, with warm breezes blowing. People would think they were lovers, she thought as his lips touched hers, perhaps even honeymooners.

As his arms closed around her, and hers rested lightly on his back, Kathy relaxed, and wondered what it would be like to honeymoon here. She didn't care at all what people thought.

Chapter Thirteen

Several days later, Kathy stood before a podium at the Federal Building in Miami in a white uniform, her gold Surface Warfare officer insignia and service ribbons shining brightly, long dark hair tucked behind her neck in a regulation bun. Hot television lights bathed the stage, making her uncomfortable. This hadn't been her idea.

". . . and how did you end up in charge of this ship full of twenty million dollars' worth of cocaine, Lieutenant?"

The question, in a woman's voice, came from behind the blinding lights of a noontime news conference. Kathy couldn't see the questioner, or the several television cameras that faced her in the large room. From the noise, she reckoned several dozen media people were out there.

"Just lucky, I guess," Kathy said, trying not to seem flippant.

She'd been told by the Task Force commander to come and tell the story of the great Navy–Coast Guard drug bust. The admiral had been pleasant; he understood she didn't want to be interviewed. He asked her to do the news conference anyway, for "the good of the service." That had settled the matter.

The media chuckled, and she continued. "The CO of the capturing Navy ship picks people to take charge. Originally, our orders were simply to sail *Marialena* into port and turn it over to the Drug Enforcement Administration."

"But that's not what happened," the voice persisted. "You sailed into a shoot-out with drug smugglers."

"We didn't anticipate that at the start," Kathy answered. "Additional intelligence became available about where the ship had been headed for a rendezvous with smugglers. Naturally, we had to pursue that lead."

"Can you tell us how you obtained this additional intelligence?"

"No, I can't," Kathy said.

She wanted to give Susan Thomas credit for finding the marked chart, but there was no sense tipping off the drug crowd about how stupid they'd been. Ignorance might help another drug gang make the same mistake again.

"We understand you rammed and sank one of the drug boats. Would you tell us about that?"

Kathy began to perspire under the hot lights.

"Both boats took us under fire when we approached them. They must have become suspicious when we didn't answer their questions as they liked. The best way to stop half the bad guys from firing at my people was to sink one boat. The wooden hull was the easier target."

". . . and you dumped its crew into shark-infested waters?" a sharp voice rang out.

Kathy took an instant dislike to the question and the questioner.

"That bunch of gangsters tried to kill my men and women out there," she snapped. "Do you think they'd care for one minute if *we* were eaten by sharks?" Her eyes flashed at the questioner behind the lights.

A buzz went through the crowd of media. Her face felt

flushed. She was fighting mad, and knew that she must cool down.

"You had *women* on this operation?" a surprised male voice asked.

Kathy paused before answering.

"In case you hadn't noticed..." she said. The room exploded in an uproar of laughter.

When the mirth subsided, Kathy continued. "Petty Officer Susan Thomas here"—she gestured—"was our navigator. She can also lay down a field of fire with an M-14 rifle as well as a Marine. Susan's not a sailor to mess with."

Kathy thought for an instant of QM1 Weatherby back on *Lockwood*. Maybe he'd learned that another way.

"We heard you were shot, Lieutenant."

"Someone tried, but didn't succeed. They put some mileage on my flak jacket, though."

"How does it feel to be a hero, Lieutenant, or perhaps I should say heroine?" an anonymous voice said.

"That's your word. I feel very humble. The people here with me today, and the rest of my crew, are your real heroes."

"Where will you go from here?" a reporter asked.

"Back to my ship, the frigate USS *Lockwood*."

"We hear the CIA was involved. Can you comment about that?"

So *that's* who the other two were in Key West, Kathy thought.

"I wouldn't know about that. No one ever said that to me."

"What did it feel like when your ship was being torn up by drug smugglers with machine guns," a reporter asked, "knowing they might try to board you and recover all that dope?"

"I was frightened that we'd all be killed. You just have to get past that and do your job."

"Anything you'd like to say, Lieutenant, in your own words?"

"Yes. I'm very grateful that we all came back safely. If I ever have to go to war, these are the people I want with me. I love them all. Now, if you'll excuse me, I have business to attend to in Key West. Lieutenant Ed Morse from the Coast Guard, who was out there with us is and commanded our armed guard, is here to answer your other questions. Thank you very much."

The whir of camera motor drives and the blinding light of flash units continued for several seconds as she left the platform.

Kathy ducked out the door, with Roy behind her. They headed for a white Navy sedan in the parking lot.

"What's this important business in Key West?" he asked as they headed for the car. He looked back to ensure that no reporters or camera crews followed them.

"Dinner with you tonight, of course," she said. "We must get back in time to change into civvies for another sunset at Mallory Dock."

"You'll have to pardon me, Lieutenant," he said, "but there's something I've been meaning to do all day." He took his hat off, set it deliberately on top of the government sedan, and drew her to him. When he kissed her, Roy's strong arms held her so well that she couldn't get away if she wanted to. She didn't want to anyway.

A car horn blared and a group of young people waved and cheered as they drove by. Nothing like being kissed in a public parking lot at high noon, in front of God and everyone, she thought.

"Why don't we talk about this some more in Key West?" she said.

Kathy felt her face flush as it hadn't in a long time, perhaps ever.

"Yes," he said, "why don't we?"

The Coast Guard had flown them by helicopter to Miami from Key West, and had offered to fly them back. Ed

Morse again came over after they'd arrived this morning and invited Kathy to dinner that night. She'd said that she was tied up with Roy.

Suddenly, she had two competitors for the evening meal. Morse was now as ready as Roy to take her hand. But Roy had seized the initiative, she thought, and captured her fancy as well.

Chapter Fourteen

"We could have taken the Coast Guard up on their offer of a helicopter ride back to Key West. Driving through the Keys is too scenic to miss, though," Roy said as they sped down I-95 toward US-1 south from Miami in a government sedan. "They sure seemed eager to please."

"Well," Kathy replied, "we delivered one of their largest drug hauls in a while, thanks to you and the crew."

"Come on, Captain," he said. "You're being too modest."

When she turned to remind him that she was no longer captain of anything, he smiled.

"Okay, okay. You're not the boss anymore, but we all enjoyed it while you were," Roy said. "Sam Apriliou says you're the first skipper he's had in combat since Vietnam. He wants to go with you on the next boarding party. The old gunner gives out no freebies. He respects you, Kathy, and so does the chief, and Boats Johnson . . . and so do I."

When she looked toward Roy, his eyes engaged hers.

"Unfortunately," Roy said, "I was stuck out of the action down there in the engine room. When we felt you crunch that wooden hull, the noise sounded like you hit a skyscraper. After you called for 'all back full' I wasn't sure whether we or the fishing boat was in trouble.''

''Being boss makes you humble in a hurry when you realize how many people you owe,'' she said.

Roy chuckled. ''We both know how that works.''

Kathy decided to enjoy the ride back to Key West as Roy drove over the fourteen-mile bridge. They saw the Gulf of Mexico and the Atlantic Ocean where they met. She and the crew had agreed to occupy the *Marialena* for a few more days until the Drug Enforcement Administration hired a contractor to keep the ship afloat.

As they reached Marathon, partway down the Keys, Roy stopped talking and his face turned serious.

''What's the matter?'' Kathy said.

''I'm eyeballing a green sedan with some men in it that's been back there since Miami. Probably nothing. How about lunch? We made such a fast break from that news conference that we didn't even get a glass of water.''

''Sounds good,'' she replied.

''Seafood?'' he asked.

''Great.''

The car threw gravel onto the highway as he turned into a combination boat yard and restaurant. The place looked promising, she thought.

''Let's take our time,'' he said as he opened the door for her, looking carefully around the parking lot.

''Sure,'' she replied.

The gregarious Greek owner, with a smiling, swarthy face and a black mustache, said that he had served in the Hellenic navy. He asked if Roy were assigned to a ship, and looked quizzically at Kathy when he learned both of them were on a frigate.

Fresh fish was preceded by *kalimarakia*, a crunchy seafood appetizer of fried squid. The owner brought over a chilled bottle of Greek white wine called *Demestica*.

"Shouldn't we be getting back, Roy?" Kathy asked after an hour and a half.

"There's no hurry. We'll be in Key West well before sunset. Mallory Dock is our objective, unless you'd like someplace else."

"Mallory Dock sounds just fine," she said.

Roy looked around carefully as they left the restaurant, and opened the door of the car for her. She noticed he again scanned the area.

He pulled the government car out onto US-1. The light breeze and the seventy-five-degree weather through the open windows blew through her hair. She leaned her head back, stretched, and closed her eyes. What a wonderful place, what a great day, now that the news conference was finished. The next few days would be hers, theirs. Then she, Roy, and the crew would join the ship when it returned to Mayport, a day's drive north from Key West.

They drove south for another thirty minutes. Roy's eyes darted frequently to the rearview mirror.

"What's wrong?" she asked.

"That green sedan's back there again. When I pulled into the seafood restaurant, they drove on by, but must have waited to pick us up when we came out. It's no coincidence. I should have called the cops when we were back there." His jaw tightened.

"Do you think they might be drug people?" Kathy asked. "Are there any police stations we can drive into?"

"Let's assume the worst. The nearest Monroe County sheriff's substation I know is far down into the Keys from here. I don't want to risk driving that far. Some pretty isolated stretches of road between here and there. They might make their move before we can find help."

"What if we gun it," she said, "and hope the police stop us for speeding? We could tell the cops the problem. They'd at least have a radio."

"Good idea, but I've seldom seen any along US-1 until we get farther south into the more inhabited keys. Meanwhile, we'll have to take our chances. I'd crowd those people off the road in a heartbeat after what they almost did to you.''

He took her hand, squeezed it lightly, and then looked forward again. ''I sure didn't mean for a pleasant afternoon to turn into a nightmare,'' he said.

''Not your fault,'' she said. ''After that last crowd of drug smugglers, we can handle anything.''

Who were the people back there? she wondered. Drug cartel operatives seeking revenge after the seizure of their ship? Would they show the American authorities they could kill people like her and Roy with impunity, that no one could confiscate one of their ships and get away with it? Or would she and Roy be damaging witnesses in the trial of the crews, troublesome obstacles to be eliminated?

''If they're bad guys, we're dead unless we lose them,'' Roy said.

''What if they're Feds, FBI, or DEA people sent to protect us?''

''Why wouldn't the Feds tell us before putting on a tail? Sure looks like a problem to me. I should have called the cops back in Marathon when we stopped for lunch.''

''What should we do?'' she asked.

''Shaking them won't be easy around here. Our only chance is the Key deer protection area near Big Pine Key.''

''What do you mean?''

''The speed limit's thirty-five there. We'll breeze on through at sixty. If the sheriff doesn't spot us, we'll head off into the protection area and cut through residential side streets. I was down here some years ago. There's a road that will take us farther south if worse comes to worst. That's my best shot.''

Kathy resisted the temptation to look back. She pulled the compact out of her purse and used the mirror to see that there was, indeed, a green car behind them.

''We haven't been out of trouble since we took over the *Marialena*, have we?'' she said.

"No, but, shucks, who wants to lead a dull life?" He looked again into the mirror, then put his foot to the floor. The car surged forward.

"Or a short one, either," Kathy replied with a sigh. "Go for it, Roy." *Not that we have any real choice.*

KEY DEER AREA, SPEED LIMIT 35 MPH, the sign said. Roy, she noticed, was clocking 55. The green sedan behind them dropped back and still had them in sight, she thought.

"Okay, we're coming into Big Pine Key. I'll make a sharp right at the traffic light, then we'll gun it. I can lose them on side roads if we pull far enough ahead."

Traffic slowed and bunched up as they came into the inhabited area that occupied both sides of the road. Roy slowed slightly. Kathy saw the red light and the cluster of traffic ahead of them.

"Roy!" she said.

"Hang on, Kathy," he replied, then cut to the right onto the narrow shoulder. Gravel crunched as he roared down the uneven path and missed cars on his left by inches. The car swayed as he roared around the corner, tires squealing, the rear end fishtailing, his foot to the floor now. The car flew down a road with houses on their left and tall vegetation on the right, both a blur. Less than a minute later, he swung sharply left, down a rutted road, then right, then left again.

"I hope the dust settles enough so they can't follow us," he said. The roads had been a mixture of pavement and sand.

"Is there any way out of here?" she asked.

"Beats me. Not exactly my neighborhood."

A sandy road led off to the left.

"I'm heading down here," he said. "That will pull us out of sight. Even if they double back, they'll have a tough time finding us."

Ten minutes later Roy persuaded a local family to let him use their phone. He called FBI Miami and told them the story.

"I've talked to everyone in the office," he said to Kathy, frustrated.

"You're who?" he said into the phone.

There was a pause.

"Oh, you're the special agent in charge. Do I have to repeat the whole story again?" He listened for a while.

"They were who?" Roy's voice dropped.

He put his hand over the phone.

"Those people back there were FBI," Roy said to Kathy. "They're looking all over for us.

"Well, next time," he spoke to the receiver, "tell us before you send your agents to tail us. We thought they were drug dealers trying to eliminate potential witnesses. If we were armed, someone could have been hurt, or killed."

He seemed to listen to some additional words over the phone.

"They were supposed to have contacted us, let us know they were there," he said, his hand over the receiver.

Roy's face was red, his voice angry.

"I expect you'll have some words with whoever led that detail," he said. "We don't want to go through this again."

The usually calm, easygoing Roy was on the thin edge of rage, she thought. That was okay. They deserved it. His low-key nature hid a hard-nosed, tough-minded warrior, she thought.

He thanked the lady of the house where they'd used the phone and slipped some bills from his wallet under the phone.

"Let them pick us up again, if they can," he said as they drove away, back toward US-1. "They might even think we've headed back north until they get the radio message. Perhaps they'll even back off."

"You were very restrained, Roy, under the circumstances."

"More than you would have been?"

"I'd say so." She smiled at him. "Irish temper."

"Remind me not to get you angry."

"Not likely . . . not any time soon," she said, patting his shoulder. As they rode south, Kathy saw no sign of the FBI car.

She leaned her head back and felt the tension drain away when Roy drove past Boca Chica. In another twenty minutes, he said, they'd be in Key West.

Chapter Fifteen

The salty morning breeze from the Atlantic was soft and easy to take, Kathy thought. She and Roy waited on the pier at the Mayport Naval Station as USS *Lockwood* approached the dock. Chief Varsik, Boats Johnson, Gunner Apriliou, and the other prize crewmembers milled around nearby.

The crew would be anxious for liberty after three weeks at sea, she thought. She wondered how the women on board had fared, if Weatherby had been foolish enough to make a move on any others.

She recalled the idyllic week in Key West, where she and Roy had moved to the bachelor officers quarters downtown after they turned the *Marialena* over to DEA's contractor. They'd walked around the town, visited nearby keys, and enjoyed every good restaurant they could find. Several evenings, hand in hand, they had watched the sunset from Mallory Dock.

"Probably the only paid 'skating' you'll have during your career," he'd said.

Once the ship tied up, the two officers went aboard to report to the XO.

"The message traffic's been interesting," Levine said. "Sounds like a John Wayne or Wonder Woman script. CHINFO sent us a transcript of your news conference, Kathy. You sure didn't give those reporters much slack."

Kathy smiled.

"What matters," she said, "is the job our people did. I'll submit award recommendations in the next few days. We're not still 'budgeting' medals around here, are we?"

"I don't think so," Levine said with a wry smile. "Not now, anyway.

"Roy," he continued, "you did good work keeping that antique steaming long enough to get into port, especially after your engine room fire."

"That credit goes to Chief Varsik," Hobbs said.

"But if the old ship broke down, or worse," Levine said, "we'd be asking you two why. Unfortunately, however, the honeymoon is over. You prize crew folks have just joined the duty section for our first day in port. Not wonderful gratitude, but . . ." He shrugged.

"We understand, XO," Kathy said.

"By the way, Jack Goldhaver was out of the hospital in Jacksonville after two days of X rays and observation. Chief Andrews and 'Doc' Fiori did a good surgical job on him."

"Did Jack *really* insist on having some medicinal alcohol before they took that bullet out?" Kathy asked.

"Of course he did," the XO said dryly. "The hole wasn't in his head." They all laughed.

Kathy stood to leave.

"One more thing, Kathy," the XO said, his face serious now. "Actually, two other things. Weatherby tried it again."

"Who . . . ?"

"Fiori," the XO replied. "The 'doc' almost took him apart after he pawed her. She kicked and scratched him something fierce. I can hardly believe it of that quiet, soft-spoken . . ."

"Remember, XO," Kathy said, "Fiori was the one who had Jack's pistol during the firefight while she patched him up. She was ready to shoot anyone who threatened him."

"I should have remembered that," he said. "The other good news is that Ward saw the whole thing, and will testify against Weatherby at the court-martial."

"One first-class petty officer testifying against another? A court-martial? We *have* come a long way," she said.

"Ward's a pretty straight-up guy, as you know. Fiori draws a lot of water with the crew after she fixed up Goldhaver under fire. The troops know she's gutsy, and they like that."

"You said there were two things, XO."

"We also solved the problem of Weatherby's replacement. A second class quartermaster named Susan Thomas will take over as leading petty officer."

"Second class . . . Susan passed the exam and got rated?"

"Yes. By the way, Kathy, the old man was the one who wanted Weatherby off his ship. He referred him over for court-martial after captain's mast. I think he understands the problem now."

"Well, I'll be . . ."

Levine smiled, but said nothing more as she and Roy left the XO's stateroom.

Later, after most of the crew had gone ashore on liberty, Roy walked into the weapons office, where Kathy sat working on reports that had piled up while she was away.

"Hi," he said. He closed the door and kissed her on the side of the neck.

"Hi," she replied. She put her hand out to touch his.

"Here we are in the fishbowl."

"It wasn't a fishbowl when we left."

"True. I guess our viewpoint has changed."

"We do have to be careful, Roy. I can't send any signals that would make this mixed-manning experiment go wrong," she said. "I can just see *Lockwood* being nicknamed the 'Love Boat' after all the women decide to have shipboard boyfriends because their woman officer has one."

"I understand that," Roy said. "I also suspect that one John Taylor wouldn't mind having this demonstration fail."

"I won't give him that satisfaction," she said.

"Everyone will know about us sooner or later," he said.

"That's not important, Roy. As long as we don't cause problems aboard ship . . ."

"Are you saying that we'll have to stop meeting like this?"

"No, only that we should be smart. No one will see you come out of my stateroom, for instance, because you won't ever be in my stateroom. Things like that," she said.

"We could have worse problems, like one of us being deployed to the Mediterranean for six months. Let's deal with what we have." He kissed her again.

"I have to go," he said.

She took his hand and squeezed it. Then he turned, and closed the door behind him.

Kathy decided to turn in early, at least to stretch out on her bunk after eight-o'clock reports at 7:30 P.M. The long drive from Key West to Mayport yesterday had followed a series of busy days. She'd reluctantly agreed to interviews with several magazines and the Associated Press, and hoped the spotlight would disappear now.

She tried to doze, but couldn't. The thought of Roy's kiss and embrace in the weapons office earlier today warmed her.

It was always something with men, Kathy thought. She recalled the young civilian engineer she'd met at a party in Annapolis when she was a firstclassman at the Academy.

Ken Lodge had been charming and sincere. His dark hair and blue eyes were like her own, but he was three inches taller. Since he was an MIT electrical engineer, the two had a lot in common. Both thrived on classical music, soft-shell crabs, and quiet times together. Ken's job with an Annapolis consulting firm kept him traveling around the state, but he'd almost always returned for the weekends during her senior year.

When he'd first kissed her two weeks after they met, her knees felt weak, her face flushed. She wondered if that was what being in love was all about. They took long walks in the brisk fall air that year. He'd called daily when she went home to New York on Christmas leave.

They talked about everything, except her career intentions. Perhaps he'd waited for her to tell him in her own way. He'd described his ambitions one night in the early spring, about his dream to open his own firm. He clearly wanted to know about hers.

"I plan to stay in the Navy," she'd said finally. "I want to command a destroyer, have the same full-spectrum career that only men have had up to now."

"How will you do that and have a normal life, too?" he'd asked.

"How do *men* lead normal lives? Am I less entitled to one than anyone else?"

"I'm talking about the 'mommy track,' your husband's career, how you balance all these things with a peripatetic life of going to sea and moving around the world."

"I didn't say a Navy career would be easy, only that it's what I want. I don't have all the answers yet." She'd avoided saying she was in no hurry to marry.

His face had registered disappointment. Kathy knew she should have said this earlier, but she'd been having too much fun and didn't want to face questions for which she mightn't be able to stand the answers. She chided herself for selfishness and lack of courage. The relationship faded rapidly, and had withered by the time graduation rolled around.

Several of her classmates were being married in the Naval Academy chapel during the week after graduation, but none were women. A year and a half later, she'd received an invitation to Ken's wedding to a local Annapolis girl, a young woman he'd never have to worry about going away to sea on him.

She tried to close her eyes again, but memories kept flooding back.

Then there was Dana Mansfield, the bright young medical intern, the son of one of her father's colleagues. They'd first met when she came home on Christmas leave from her Coast Guard assignment. Her dad had invited the young man's physician father to bring him to a dinner party at the 92nd Street townhouse.

Kathy and Dana talked for most of the evening, spent the following day together at Radio City, wandered around gaily decorated midtown Manhattan, and even rode back and forth to Staten Island on the ferry.

"Thought you might feel at home here," he'd said as he put his arm around her on the ferry. They faced the icy breeze blowing across New York Harbor as the huge boat steamed past the Statue of Liberty on its way to Staten Island.

"It's sort of a busman's holiday, but easy when you're not responsible for the ship. Besides, the cutter I'm on is smaller than this—more fun to play around with."

Their eyes had met then, both tearing from the stiff wind. He put his hand to her face and kissed her gently.

"Like to go inside?" he asked, taking her hand.

"No, let's stay out here for a while. We become spoiled by steam heat and comfort, get dried out by artificial things. The wind is cold, but it's fresh, and untamed."

"You're tough, Kathy," Dana had said, "but that's good. It's a hard life." He wrapped his arm around her shoulder, bent, and kissed her lightly again. When they docked in Staten Island, he held her hand as they walked around the St. George area near the terminal. They ate in a small local restaurant, then rode back to Manhattan, this time inside the ferry's large passenger cabin.

That night, Kathy knew she'd have to tell Dana about her career intentions soon, and not let things go as far as they had last time. Dana was a wonderful man, a sweet man. Any other way wasn't honest, she thought.

But here it was two years later, and she hadn't done that.

Kathy heard the single bell announcing 8:30 P.M., and knew she was no closer to dozing than she had been.

At least Roy understood what she wanted. He probably knew her better as a human being than the previous men in her life. Roy knew the problems of Navy life like none of the others. Surely, he would have no misgivings.

Chapter Sixteen

Two weeks later, the ship was again at sea on the Caribbean drug interdiction patrol. Kathy sat at the desk in her stateroom doing paperwork when the phone buzzed.

"Come up when you can, Kathy," the XO said. "I have exciting news for you." She'd sent award recommendations that had included everyone from Roy to Chief Varsik and Boats Johnson and Susan Thomas to the CO a week before.

When she walked into Levine's office, he handed her a naval message from the commander in chief of the Atlantic Fleet.

"Congratulations, Kathy . . . not that this comes as any great surprise," the XO said.

She took the message and read it.

FM: CINCLANTFLT NORFOLK VA
TO: USS LOCKWOOD
INFO: CNO WASHINGTON DC
      COMMAVSURFLANT NORFOLK VA
      COMCRUDES GRU TWELVE

COMDESRON TWELVE

BT

UNCLAS/EFTO//NO5700//

AWARD PRESENTATION ICO LTJG KATHLEEN ANN SHANNON, USN

1. CINCLANTFLT WISHES TO PRESENT THE LEGION OF MERIT PERSONALLY TO LTJG SHANNON FOR ACHIEVEMENT IN CONNECTION WITH SEIZURE OF DRUG VESSEL SS MARIALENA AND ASSOCIATED DRUG INTERDICTION OPERATIONS. REQUEST MAKE SUBJ OFFICER AVAILABLE FOR CEREMONY AT CINCLANTFLT HQ AT 1000 LOCAL TIME 15 OCTOBER.

2. ACCTING DATA FOR SUBJ TRAVEL BY SEPMSG.

BT

"Wow," she said.

"They must want to high-profile this drug seizure. This sounds like something decided in Washington, although the CINC, Admiral Chase, is very people-oriented," Levine replied.

"We'll be in port then" she replied. "I'd sure like to take people like Varsik, Johnson, Thomas . . ."

". . . and Roy Hobbs?" Levine offered.

"Yes, and Roy, of course, XO." She hadn't wanted to lead with him.

"There probably won't be enough money for that. They'll likely only allocate enough for a round-trip airline ticket to Norfolk and per diem for you," Levine said.

"You know," she said, "CINCLANTFLT approves all those awards for the crew. If Admiral Chase is as people-oriented as you say, he might want to decorate the other people, too. The people in Norfolk who came up with the idea might find this a nice add-on."

"You're really pushing this," the XO said. "But our people deserve it. Maybe I can make some phone calls and try to get LANTFLT to make this *their* great idea."

"What if we drove a government van and gave the others

permissive temporary duty orders? We could house everyone on the base up there. The trip wouldn't cost the ship
anything.''

"I'll try that out on the old man if LANTFLT adopts
your idea.''

When she looked up, Levine was smiling.

Kathy wondered when the CO would sign out the award
recommendations she'd already finished and sent forward.
All Commander Taylor had to do was approve them. Perhaps that was why Jeff Levine had smiled, because this
message upped the ante. Taylor had done her out of one
award, she thought. He couldn't do her out of this one, and
wouldn't do any of her people out of the ones they deserved, if she could help it.

The Marine guard saluted smartly as the gray government van, with Boats Johnson at the wheel and Roy in the
front passenger seat, drove through the Naval Base gate at
Norfolk, Virginia at 3:30 P.M. the day before the award
ceremony. Kathy, Susan Thomas, Chief Varsik, and Gunner Apriliou sat in the back seats.

After they dropped off the other men and Susan Thomas,
Kathy went to the Atlantic Fleet headquarters building. She
wanted to confirm the time and arrangements with Admiral
Chase's staff.

"Come over about twenty minutes before the ceremony,'' the CINC's executive assistant, or EA, told her.
"The boss wants to talk to you privately.''

"Is that usual, Captain?'' she asked. Busy four-star ad-
mirals, she thought, had little time for socializing with junior-grade lieutenants.

"No, it's quite unusual,'' the EA replied. "The admiral
specifically asked to see you.''

When she appeared the following morning in her best
blue uniform, the captain ushered her into a large room
with thick carpeting and a large oak desk. The sturdy, gray-

haired man with gold stripes halfway up the sleeve of his dress blue coat seemed about her father's age. He looked up and smiled, then rose and walked over to greet her, his large hand extended. Admiral Harry Chase commanded every U.S. Navy ship from Norfolk to the European continent.

"I've wanted to meet the officer who whipped that bunch of drug smugglers with an old freighter," he said with a broad smile. He took her hand in both of his, then motioned toward a pair of large leather chairs.

"Lieutenant Shannon, I want to tell you, aside from all the starchy formalities of today's ceremony, what a super job you did. Your decision to ram that drug boat was first-rate combat sailoring."

"The people outside deserve most of the credit, Admiral. I'm grateful to you for decorating them at the same time."

The admiral surveyed her silently for a moment.

"Giving credit to your subordinates is a fine officerlike quality, and so is modesty. In the end, though, you were in command, the one who gave the orders. If people were killed, or your ship were lost, or that engine room fire burned out of control, you'd have the tall explaining to do."

Kathy nodded.

"Command of a prize crew is a big job for a twenty-four-year-old junior-grade lieutenant," Chase continued. "Your skipper must think very highly of you."

She looked down. If he only knew.

"Tell me, how did you figure out the rendezvous point with the other drug boats? That really clinched it."

"The third-class quartermaster you'll decorate this morning searched the navigation space on the freighter and found the chart with markings on it. I contacted the Coast Guard cutter assigned to escort us in. We didn't make that fact public, not even in Susan Thomas's award citation."

"So the next crowd of drug thugs can screw it up the same way, eh?"

"Something like that, sir."

"*Susan* Thomas," he said. It was the admiral's turn to nod. "Smart," he said, "very smart."

He paused for a moment and stroked his chin.

"That combat with the drug smugglers was as close to war as most people get," he said. "You said during the news conference in Miami that you were frightened."

"Yes, sir. For a while, I thought we'd all be killed."

Chase leaned back in his chair and looked her in the eye.

"Being frightened isn't what matters, you know. It's how you conquer the fear and carry on. You did the right thing—went on the offensive, brought the battle to the enemy. I'm very proud of you."

He knows about combat, she thought. Everyone knew the Navy Cross on Chase's ribbon bar had been won as a fighter pilot in Vietnam.

"My people were some of those "sailormen in battle fare since fighting days of old,' Admiral," she said softly, recounting words from the Naval Academy hymn.

"This country will survive only as long as we have people like that," he said quietly.

Kathy nodded.

"There's another reason I wanted to see you," he said. "I have a job coming open on my personal staff soon for a tough-minded, warfare-qualified officer. I expect that your brand of courage includes speaking your mind, even telling the old man if you think he's wrong. That's what I need. Are you interested?"

Kathy agonized, hesitating for a moment.

"Your offer's very flattering, sir. I'm also three months into the mixed-crew test program on *Lockwood*. The future of women in small combatants may depend on how that turns out. I feel obligated to finish what I started. I hope you understand, Admiral."

"I expected you to say that. There'll be a good job here for you after you complete that tour, if you want it."

"Thank you, sir." Kathy swallowed hard.

"That's no freebie. People only get what they earn around here," he said. "I want you to get in touch with me before you're ready for orders. I mean that." The tone of his voice left no doubt.

Chase looked at his watch. "I think we have an appointment with some other folks outside," he said. He walked toward the door to the conference room, pulled it open, and gestured to Kathy to go ahead.

When she stepped in, the room was full of people. One of the first faces she saw, standing next to her father, was that of Dr. Dana Mansfield.

Chapter Seventeen

Kathy watched as Admiral Chase's aide read each of the citations, starting with Susan Thomas, the most junior of the group to be decorated. Chase spoke to each recipient after pinning on the medal, and shook hands. Boats Johnson and Chief Varsik wore dress blue uniforms with gold rating stripes and rows of ribbons marking long, eventful careers. The gold recognized at least twelve successive years of good conduct. A photographer snapped pictures.

When Kathy's turn came, Chase lifted the enameled red-and-white medal from its leather box and fastened it near her gold Surface Warfare insignia. "I meant it about the job," he whispered as he shook her hand.

"I won't forget, sir," she said, smiling. Whether the job ever worked out or not, it was flattering to be asked.

"Why don't you and Lieutenant Hobbs join me for lunch in the flag mess?" the admiral said. "I see your dad here, and that other fellow. Bring them along, too."

When the ceremony ended, Kathy hugged her father and Dana Mansfield. The two had flown into Norfolk that morning. They'd fly to New York at five-fifteen and be back in operating rooms tomorrow morning.

Dana's hug was warmer and stronger than she expected.

"What a wonderful surprise to see you here," she said.

"I wouldn't have missed today for anything. Not every day do I get to congratulate a real heroine."

"You've been watching too much TV news," she said.

"Sometimes we define ourselves when we confront a tough situation," Dana said.

Roy joined them after he congratulated Varsik and Johnson.

"This is Roy Hobbs. He became an on-the-job expert with antique steam engines and damage control and brought the ship back to Key West."

"With just a few middling distractions," Roy added, smiling. "A pleasure to meet you, Dr. Shannon," he said as he took the older man's hand. When he shook hands with Dana, Kathy thought Roy might be sizing up the young surgeon.

"For the record, Dr. Shannon," Roy said, "Kathy was the reason we brought the ship back. She's underplayed the little matter of drug thugs and a major shoot out. The citation read today only tells the bare bones of the story. Kathy's a first-rate warrior."

"That's strange praise to give a woman, Roy," Dr. Shannon said.

"It's a great compliment for an officer, sir."

"I should have considered that. You're a real iron butterfly, Kathy," her father said as he clasped his arm around her shoulder. "You're feminine and beautiful on the outside, hard and determined on the inside. That's a winning combination, and I'm very, very proud of you.

"Well," her father continued, "everyone's surely worked up a good appetite after all this morning's excitement. Where's the best place in town for lunch?"

"The admiral's already thought of that. He's invited us all to lunch in his mess," she said.

"Kathy," her father said, "how will you ever go back to that 'tin can' of yours after all this high living?"

"Easy, Dad. In fact, I'd rather be there now, without all this folderol."

Kathy and her father walked down the narrow passageway outside the conference room together as the others followed.

"Did your mother know about this today?" her father asked.

"Yes, but she had to be in Detroit for a meeting that couldn't be changed. I'll see her when I come up next time."

"Why not come home for a few days soon, get away from things, and enjoy yourself?" her father said.

"I'll do that," she said. "It should be easier to get a leave chit approved now that the CO is in a good mood. At least he ought to be, but who can tell?"

Admiral Harry Chase could be charming when he wanted to be, she'd heard, and tough as hardtack when he had to be. Now, he engaged her father and Dana in conversation.

"I'm glad Kathy and Roy are making the Navy a career," Chase said. "We need smart, tough-minded people. Life's more complex in the fleet than ever. Drug interdiction is only one of our many challenges."

Dana didn't react when the admiral said that, she thought, as though he hadn't heard it, or wished he hadn't.

After lunch, Kathy and Roy toured her father and Dana along the piers at the massive naval base. She pointed out a ship of *Lockwood*'s class.

"Nothing like the *Marialena* down here to show us?" her father asked, a smiling glint in his eye.

"No, thank heaven," she replied. "The *Marialena* looked like a wreck by the time we brought it in."

When they finished the tour, Dr. Shannon glanced at his

watch. "We'd better head for the airport. Time has really flown by."

"Why don't you ride with your dad and Dana?" Roy said. "I'll follow in the van and take you back to the base."

"Thanks, that's a thoughtful idea," Kathy said.

As her father drove to the airport, Kathy and Dana sat next to him in the front seat.

"Thanks for letting me share this special day, Kathy," Dana said. "I really enjoyed it."

"It was great to see you both here."

When they arrived at the airport, Dana turned and kissed her. His lips were warm, his embrace as close as he'd ever held her, here in broad daylight, in front of everyone. Perhaps he was sending messages, different messages, to her, her father, even to Roy.

"You're coming up to New York soon, I hope?" Dana asked.

"In a couple of weeks, when I come back from sea again."

"Great, we can always take another ride on the Staten Island ferry if you get homesick . . . or is it seasick?"

Both laughed.

"I'll have my fill of sea for a while by then," she said.

"I do miss you when you're away, Kathy," Dana whispered. "It will be so good to spend some time together."

"Yes," she said as the embrace ended. "Yes, it will."

As they drove back to the base later, Kathy noticed Roy was quiet. He said nothing about Dana's passionate kiss at the airport before the young doctor walked into the terminal. She must have a serious talk with Dana when she went home, and resolve where they stood once and for all.

"Well, back to Florida early tomorrow morning," Roy said. "Good that we have enough people to share the driving."

"It's been a super day," she said. "Glad Admiral Chase

worked it out so everyone could share the glory side of this, too. He really cares about the people.''

"I'm glad *we* could share it," Roy said.

"Yes, there was enough good time for everyone, wasn't there?''

Chapter Eighteen

Falling leaves littered the Manhattan sidewalk as Kathy stepped from the cab near her father's townhouse on 92nd Street off Fifth Avenue. The mid-October breeze was cool, the sun strong, as she paid the driver for the ride from Kennedy Airport. Next time, she thought, she'd fly into Newark to avoid midtown's traffic gridlock.

She hadn't seen most of her family and friends in four months, and needed a break. After the drug bust and work on the *Lockwood*, Kathy was ready for a few days of sleeping late. Also there was a decision to make about Dana and Roy.

Her father embraced her when he answered the door. "We didn't have nearly enough time to talk during that quick trip to Norfolk," he said, kissing her cheek. "We'll make up for that, now that you're home."

Kathy wasn't sure how her father might react to Roy. If he were a surgical resident, she thought, there'd be no question. But a naval officer, although no surprise, would be another thing.

She decided not to mention that she'd been looking over

her shoulder since the drug seizure and was sensitive to being followed. The tense ride from Miami to Key West had fixed the idea in her mind. The FBI had told her to call the local field office immediately if she detected surveillance.

She reached into the side pocket of her luggage. "Here's a videotape of the press conference, in case you'd like to see the rest of the story one of these days," she said.

"Great, we can watch that together later. I have some friends coming for dinner tonight, including a young man you know."

"Dana?"

"Yes, of course. I think you really have his attention, Kathy."

She walked up the stairs and into her own room and kicked off her shoes. A few minutes later, a knock on the door stirred her from a catnap. Maggie O'Neill, her father's housekeeper since just after the divorce when Kathy was ten, came in. A widow, Maggie generally spoke little, and always softly.

" 'Tis good to see you, Miss Kathleen," she said, the lilt of an Irish brogue in her voice. "And wonderful to have you in the house again."

Maggie called her by her proper name, and had taught her the finer points of manners in dealing with older and more distinguished people. Kathy jumped up and hugged the older woman tightly. She was more like an aunt, sometimes a surrogate mother. "Maggie, it's great to see you, too. It's seemed so long since I've been home."

"You're away leading your own life now, lass. Don't be apologizing for that. Great things, too, you've been doing, I hear."

"Nothing I'd intended. I can do very well without drug smugglers, thanks," she said.

"Your young man is coming to dinner tonight. Did your father tell you?"

"Yes, I look forward to seeing Dana," she said.

"He is a very charming fellow. Dr. Mansfield's been here several times to dinner. He's very sweet on you, Kathleen. I can see it in his eyes when he speaks of you."

"You've never missed much, Maggie." Kathy wouldn't tell her that Dana had written to her each month for the past year, long, chatty letters designed to keep his memory alive with her.

The young doctor had always been kind to Maggie, she thought. Dana's sensitivity to people was among the qualities Kathy liked in him, a virtue that would help make him successful in his profession.

After Maggie left, Kathy stretched out for a rest. Her father would likely want to watch the video tomorrow, perhaps after breakfast. Kathy had seen the tape on the ship when it first came in, and had been surprised at how confident she looked and sounded while a cloud of butterflies flew around in her stomach.

About five-thirty, Kathy took a long, warm shower, washed her long hair, and dried it slowly. Civilians didn't understand that "Hollywood" showers were forbidden aboard ship where fresh water was scarce. Her leisurely splash, once taken for granted, had become a delicious luxury.

Kathy picked out a long velvet skirt and a silk and lace blouse from her closet, and jewelry from her drawer. She combed out her hair to its full length, something else impractical at sea. Tonight would be different. In fact, all this week she'd put her cares behind her, have a good time . . . and sleep late. Only her conversation with Dana, when they were alone sometime during the next few days, concerned her.

At six-thirty, the bell rang, and Maggie let in Dana Mansfield. He hugged Kathy, and kissed her warmly on the cheek.

"You look beautiful tonight," he whispered. "Perhaps we can make up for the chat time we didn't have in Norfolk, now that you're home for a while."

"You rascal, I bet you say that to all those women residents and cute nurses. . . ."

"And here you are back from a ship with eight women among two hundred men," he parried. "I think you're spoiled by all the attention there."

"There's no time for 'attention' during a sixteen-hour day, but you residents know about that. That, and loose-fitting cotton uniforms, keeps me out of trouble."

"Yes," he said with resignation, "we both know about long hours. In fact, I'm on call tonight." He pulled a beeper from his pocket.

"Come," she said, taking his arm, "let's enjoy ourselves before that thing goes off."

"Why don't we talk about you, now that you're famous," he said.

"The glare of the TV lights and all those media interviews aren't as glamorous as they appear."

"Have you had any proposals of marriage yet?" Dana asked.

Kathy looked at him quizzically.

"Don't you know that every beautiful woman who appears on TV receives fan mail from men who want to marry her? I'm surprised you haven't had a mailbag full already."

"Sorry, no proposals yet. I guess not everyone shares your view of attractiveness. Either that or they don't know where to send the letter." She laughed.

"Well, I'm lucky that they don't," he replied, and took her hand.

"Don't which?"

"Both," he replied.

Two couples arrived minutes later. Both men were surgeons, their wives well attired, precisely coiffed, and charming. Kathy wondered about their real life beneath the refined, expensive exterior. Her own mother had found it stifling enough to bow out of, but perhaps that assessment wasn't fair.

Why didn't Dad ever invite a woman surgeon and her non-medical husband? she wondered.

The last arrival, who came from her art gallery by taxi, was Martha Winston Lake, her father's longtime companion. Martha's tailored suit covered a disciplined figure, the product of careful diet and regular exercise. Only salt-and-pepper hair reflected her forty-five years, Kathy thought, but she was still striking.

Martha came to Kathy immediately after giving Ross Shannon a peck on the cheek, and hugged her. The two women had always gotten along well together. Better, Kathy thought, than her relationship had been with her own mother over the years.

"Seagoing life seems to agree with you, Kathy," Martha said. "You look great."

"Right now being home agrees with me, too."

Kathy often wondered why Martha and her father had never married. They'd been seeing each other for ten years and seemed comfortable, compatible. She'd never asked her father about the relationship, and he'd never volunteered his feelings. That was like him, she thought. He seldom showed emotions.

A glass of wine with Dana warmed her. At seven-thirty, they sat down at a long formal table to a light supper of fish with an herb and caper sauce, wild rice, and fresh vegetables. Must be Martha's influence, she thought, and wondered how much input she had into things like this.

"You don't know how good it is to have you back, Kathy," Dana said.

Something about the candlelight made his eyes sparkle.

"It *is* nice to be home after the endless excitement of the past few weeks."

He took her hand lightly from time to time as they sat next to each other at dinner. Dana kept up a lively conversation, and gave her his full attention.

"Can you squeeze me into your date book for dinner tomorrow night?" he asked as they finished dessert.

"I think I can handle that."

"About seven? I know a great little Italian place in the Village."

"You won't be on call again, will you?"

"No, I can stay out all night tomorrow. We can watch the dawn come up on the Staten Island ferry if you like."

As dinner ended, Ross Shannon spoke.

"I'd like to show all of you this tape of Kathy's press conference in Miami after she captured the drug ship. It's only about twenty minutes. I haven't seen it yet either."

With that, he went to the cassette player atop the big-screen TV and inserted the tape. Kathy hadn't intended for him to show this to everyone. But after all, he *was* proud of what she'd done.

Afterward, Ann Hargrave, one of the surgeons' wives, said to her, "I can't believe they let a woman have this much responsibility at such a young age. How did you ever talk them into that, Kathy?"

"I didn't. My executive officer talked the captain into it."

"But no one knew what was going to happen," the woman said.

"That's true, least of all, me. Fortunately, I made enough right decisions that everything worked out as it did."

"You could have been killed," the other wife said.

"That can happen crossing the street in New York," Kathy said. "Staying alive is a matter of being as careful as you can."

"You seemed more daring than careful, Kathy," Martha said. She'd stood quietly, listening to the others.

"Careful doesn't mean passive. We had to take one drug boat out to reduce our risk. I couldn't stay there and let them both shoot at us."

The women nodded, but Kathy knew they didn't understand. That didn't matter. They'd never have to do what she'd done. The one person who'd said nothing, Kathy noticed, was Dana.

Suddenly, the persistent beep of Dana's pager interrupted them. At least he'd been able to finish dinner and enjoy part of the evening. He glanced at her with a "what can I do?" look, shrugged, and headed for the telephone.

"Sorry about this, Kathy, but you know how it is," he said as she walked him to the door. "At least we won't have to worry about interruptions tomorrow."

"There's always something to be grateful for," she said as she kissed him lightly.

He gave her a warmer, more lengthy kiss than she'd given him, and said that he'd see her the following evening.

The party broke up soon after that. Early surgery in the morning, the doctors said, except for her father, who had an operation to perform in the afternoon.

"I'll drop you off at home, Martha," Ross said. Martha smiled.

"Don't wait up, Kathy," he said. "We'll have breakfast together in the morning."

Maggie was still around, insisting on straightening up.

"Why don't those two get married, Maggie?" Kathy said after her father and Martha had left.

The older woman hesitated.

"I think it's Ms. Lake's doing. I believe your father has wanted to for some time."

She wouldn't press her further, Kathy thought.

When she turned in, Kathy couldn't sleep. She thought about Roy and Dana, about the future. Her career had taken on a steep upward curve after the successful drug seizure. Without guile or planning, she had achieved more visibility than people who'd spent years wheeling and dealing.

Kathy thought of her father, of the divorce when she was ten. Years had passed before she'd understood the deep personality differences between her parents which caused that. She had been in no hurry to fall in love, even to find a steady boyfriend. Kathy hadn't sought out Roy or Dana, but just as certainly, both seemed drawn to her.

She heard her father return at two in the morning.

* * *

When Kathy arose at eight later that morning, her father was already reading *The New York Times* with a cup of coffee in his hand and toast on the plate in front of him.

"Hi," he said. "Ready for coffee?"

She yawned and stretched in a bathrobe. "At least two cups this morning."

"Did you enjoy your reunion with Dana last night? You two didn't have much chance to talk while we were in Norfolk, or last evening, either."

"Yes, we're having dinner at some place in the Village tonight, when he's *not* on call."

"That boy's very interested in you. He's a good man and a superb surgeon. You could do much worse than Dana Mansfield."

"You don't have to sell me on him, Dad. I wish we didn't have careers heading in opposite directions."

"Kathy, you'll be a success in anything you do. You've already proven that. If you were to take up another career . . ."

"Da-ad!"

Her father slouched down slightly in his chair and took the coffee cup in both hands, leaving the newspaper open on the table.

"You won't walk into an opportunity like Dana Mansfield again. Not next week, or next year, maybe ever. In five or ten years, he'll have a place like this. What will you be doing?"

"Probably sailing on another destroyer . . ." she said quietly, and got up to pour herself another cup of coffee.

Pogo's Restaurant in the west Village was everything Dana promised, she thought. Candles in Chianti bottles provided the only light for the tables; great Italian food and romantic music created a relaxed atmosphere. The warm darkness created an aura of intimacy. Even though other couples talked and ate at tables but a few feet away, the room was quiet.

Dana ordered a bottle of white wine for them, as Kathy surveyed the menu. Accordion music played softly in the background.

After a few minutes, they ordered dinner. They talked about his life as a resident, an experience he was clearly looking to finish up in another year or so.

"It's worth it in the end," he said, "but they get their pound of flesh in the process."

She knew exactly what he wanted, that he'd made all the sacrifices his profession entailed.

"How did you ever find this place?" she asked.

Dana paused for a moment.

"Came down here with some people from the hospital one time. Got lucky."

"I'll say you did. This is terrific. What a lovely way to spend an evening."

"I've been talking a lot about my job, my intentions tonight, maybe too much. You're determined to stay in the Navy, aren't you, Kathy?"

When she looked over at him, his expression had become more serious.

"What tells you that?"

"The way you handled yourself during that news conference, the things you said to the admiral over lunch. The confident way you answered his questions. You feel deeply about what you're doing."

"You're right, I do care. What I'm doing makes a difference."

"And you do intend to stay in, too, don't you?"

"Yes. I wasn't sure at the start, but I am now." She'd intended to start this conversation, but Dana had beat her to it, she thought.

"It's not just this drug business . . ."

"And the publicity? Heck, no! That's the part I *don't*

like. I've found a rewarding profession, and a lot of very good people.''

Dana sighed, almost silently.

"I was hoping we had a chance, Kathy, for something beautiful, something long-term.''

"I wish I knew how we could, Dana, I really do.''

"What kind of life will the Navy give you? How can you have a husband, children, a normal existence as a woman, if you spend half your life at sea, and move from place to place around the world the other half? That's hard enough for a man, but it sounds impossible for a woman to do and maintain any stable relationship.''

"No one said it would be easy. My career in the Navy means as much to me as neurosurgery does to you.''

"Very few men can accommodate their careers to that,'' he said.

Kathy nodded, then looked down. "I know,'' she said.

And you're one who can't, and I can't blame you, she thought sadly. Like her relationship with Ken Lodge in Annapolis, except Dana's neurosurgery specialty made him even less flexible about moving around, once he finished his residency. No one pulled up a surgical practice and moved every couple of years.

Even if he'd agree to share her life by becoming a Navy doctor, which would involve a massive cut in income, neurosurgeons practiced at the large teaching hospitals, not the small ones at outlying bases. He'd locked himself into a course and so had she. They were headed in such different directions that they'd soon be out of sight of each other, emotionally as well as geographically.

"I care for you a lot, Kathy.'' He reached over and took her hand. "You know that. I'd like for it to be a lot more.''

"I care for you, too, Dana. It's difficult to conduct a relationship by long distance, even more difficult the more serious the relationship becomes.''

"That's what's going to happen, isn't it, that it will become too hard?''

"We're both being pulled by circumstances beyond our control."

Dana's face looked pained now.

"I don't know about that. I love you, Kathy. I've cared for you ever since we first met, when you were at the Naval Academy and I was in med school."

Kathy wasn't as surprised as she thought she'd be to hear him say that. The signals had grown less subtle these last couple of times home, and in his letters and calls.

"When people love each other," she said, "they have to be together. Even when they can be, there are no guarantees. Being apart a lot is just too big a risk factor. I wish I knew some smart way to deal with the different paths life's going to take us down, and the separation."

She thought about her parents. A lot of common interests and years together hadn't protected them from breakup.

"I wish I did, too," he said. "I guess it's conflicting priorities."

Maybe he means my priorities aren't as important, maybe he doesn't. No sense arguing about that.

"People live for more than one thing these days, at least some people do. I'd make an awful housewife, regardless of how much I loved you, if that's all I was able to do."

"I wish we could find a way to work this out. I can't ask you to give up your career in the Navy, Kathy. You must be happy with what you're doing with your life, just as I am."

"I don't have any answers either. There's no way either of us can have what we want without cutting a chunk out of the other's life. I'm sorry, Dana, very, very sorry."

"May I take you home now?" he asked quietly.

When he left Kathy at the door, he'd kissed her warmly, lingeringly. "If anything changes, I'll still be here," he said, and brushed her hair with his hand before he turned to go back to his car. Neither of them said good-bye.

Chapter Nineteen

"You did *what?*" Kathy's father said as they had coffee the following morning in the sunny breakfast nook at the back of his elegant urban townhouse.

"I told Dana I couldn't see him anymore, that our careers were headed in such different directions, that I could see no way we'd ever ..."

"The man's in love with you, Kathy. Can't you see that? Isn't that important?"

Her father stood and began to pace.

"Of course it's important, and yes, I know that. Dana is a wonderful man, and I care a lot for him, too."

Ross turned toward her.

"... but you don't love him, is that it?"

"That's not the point, Dad. I know I could love Dana. But there's nowhere for us to go ..."

"It doesn't have to be that way, Kathy," Ross said, struggling for patience.

Dana had as much as said that last night.

"No, it doesn't. All I have to do is give up a career I love, leave the Navy, marry Dana, and live happily ever

134

after. Well, I'm not like Vera Mason or Connie Appleby. I can't be content, as they are, being prominent neurosurgeons' wives. 'Catching' the right man and being taken care of for life is not what I'm about. How could marriage make me happy if I had to throw away something else I love in order to have it?''

"Look at your sister Fiona," her father said. "She fell in love and married that accountant. She could have had any number of men with more promise, and a much more comfortable life than a tract house in New Jersey, washing dishes, and changing diapers. You can fall in love with a man of means without being a scheming female, you know."

"Yes, but she's a different person than I am. After six years, Fiona's still very much in love with Harold and has two beautiful, bright children. Would any of these fellows you had picked out for her have made her this happy?''

"You're just like your mother, Kathy," Ross said. "I hate to say that, but you are."

"Because I want to have a life of my own, a career of my own in addition to marriage?''

"She had to have everything her way. That's why the marriage finally broke up."

That wasn't what her mother would say if she were here, Kathy thought.

"And you think I'm like that because I won't give up my profession for a man I could love, because I want to have a career too, that I'm selfish, willful, wrong? Sorry, Dad, I can't accept that. If you think that way, you don't understand either me or my profession."

"Kathy, I didn't mean that to hurt you. What I'm saying is that you have to make choices, you have to settle for things in this life."

"What choices have *you* made? What have *you* had to settle for? Why must the women always make the concessions, always do the settling? Why am I wrong for wanting to have both things in life, if I can?''

"You're not wrong. Dana is a special man, and a unique opportunity for you, that's all. He has a lot more going for him, for instance, than that Roy Hobbs we met down in Norfolk."

"What's wrong with Roy?" she asked, standing and facing her father. "I learned a lot about courage from him. He risked his life to save a man during the engine room fire. Despite what he said, Roy was the one who brought that ship back to port with a crippled engineering plant."

"There's nothing wrong with Roy, Kathy. Perhaps I was out of line to use him as an example. . . ."

"You bet your socks you were."

"Kathy, I want you to be happy, not spend your life chasing after things that don't bring you anything."

"Dad, I'm a big girl now."

Her father breathed deeply.

"I know that, and I didn't mean to sound critical about you being like your mother," he said. "I truly thought that Dana was the right man for you, but that's not my call. Between your profession and your love life, I'm batting zero so far."

"Maybe it's not your ball game," she said, "or maybe you're swinging too hard. What does Martha think about all this?"

"I haven't spoken to her about it, about your career and Dana, I mean. Perhaps I should."

"Try it out on her. She may agree or she may not, but she'll give you another woman's-eye view of things."

"You like Martha a lot, don't you?" he said.

"Yes, she's smart, kind, honest . . . I trust her."

"So do I, Kathy, so do I."

For a moment, Kathy wished she'd never come home. But she'd had to. Otherwise, this necessary parting with Dana mightn't have happened until much later. It would only have hurt everyone even more. She'd allowed her hopeless relationship with Ken Lodge to go on too long;

she couldn't make the same mistake again. That hadn't made it easier.

The wind blew chilly when Kathy stepped out of the townhouse later that morning to walk to the Metropolitan Museum of Art. She wanted to meander around the galleries, have time to think. Tonight, she'd have dinner with her mother, then go see her sister Fiona tomorrow.

New York was a great place to visit, she thought, but she'd enjoyed other places she'd seen, too. Kathy imagined the cities of Europe, the souks of North Africa, the pyramids, the Acropolis of Athens, and a hundred other places within her reach. Palma de Mallorca and Barcelona during midshipman summer cruises had fueled her curiosity.

As she turned the corner onto Fifth Avenue, she knew she'd never see these places as a housewife, however well placed a one. She forced the thought down. Finding a husband was not difficult. Finding the one who could share what she had, and what she did, would be harder. There'd be no hurry in her search. When she found the right man, she would know.

The museum was almost empty when she walked in. Few people wandered through the high-ceilinged galleries. After an hour of absorbing the beauty of the paintings in near silence, she sat for a moment on a bench. The only noise was the sharp clicking of a woman's high heels in the next gallery.

Her father's words about Roy Hobbs echoed through her ears. Dr. Ross Preston Shannon had spent three hours in Roy's company. He hadn't been with him through the shootout, the engine room fire, the tense drive from Miami to Key West.

Her daddy's value system keyed on financial success, that universal symbol of achievement. The pretty enameled medals on a bit of ribbon, conferred by the United States government for contributions like the drug bust, wouldn't buy a new Mercedes like Dad's.

Despite her father's reservations, Roy was the only man in her life so far with that combination of courage and tenderness. He was attractive, bright, thoughtful, and mature. Roy also seemed interested in her, at least during their time in Key West. She should have recognized these things more quickly. The right man may have been within reach all along. Roy had gone home on leave, too. Hopefully, she thought, it would not be too late to correct her mistake when she returned to the ship.

Chapter Twenty

The light traffic on I-95 told Roy Hobbs he'd make good time as he drove his four-year-old Chevy north toward home. Only a few trucks and an odd car or two sped along the plumb-straight section of road in the patchy early-morning fog. He'd pick up I-16 west at Savannah and be home in Milledgeville, Georgia, by mid-afternoon. He'd have to call Melissa Elliott when he arrived.

Kathy hadn't returned to the ship from her leave in New York. He must settle where they stood with each other when she returned. He wanted her to know of his feelings for her, a regard at which his kisses had hinted. He'd been careful, he thought, not to say too much too soon, not to frighten her off with the emotions he harbored for her.

Dana Mansfield's interest in Kathy was clear. She'd hugged the young doctor warmly when she first saw him in Norfolk, and kissed him when they parted at the airport. Competing with a handsome, articulate surgeon who'd soon earn a quarter million a year wouldn't be easy, Roy thought.

Despite how determined she seemed about the Navy,

Kathy might give up her career for the right man, he thought. Love did strange things to people, sometimes things they regretted later. Her independent spirit seemed to belie this. Being a homebody would bore her to death, he thought.

But he was headed toward another woman now, one he knew more about. The blond, easygoing Melissa was a bright, fun companion. Almost his height, her statuesque figure fit well with the lilting Southern accent that flavored her words. Her looks and personality attracted attention wherever they went. She'd developed confidence about herself since high school, and acquired a savvy sense of judgment during the years he'd known her.

Roy liked her combination of qualities, among which was being affectionate. Melissa was a small-town Southern woman, he thought, with many positive features.

More important, her mother was calm and intelligent. Roy's father had once said women's mothers told much how daughters would behave later. He'd told of several women who adopted their mothers' personalities, some to their advantage, some not.

At 2:30 P.M. Roy turned off U.S. 441 into downtown Milledgeville. In fifteen minutes he was home.

"It's wonderful to see you, Roy," his mother said, rushing to hug him as he walked in the door.

Tall and graying, Helen Hobbs hadn't seemed to change in appearance during all the years he'd known her.

Roy hadn't been home in two months; he kept finding reasons to stay in Jacksonville. He hadn't analyzed why his trips home had become so infrequent, except that they kept him closer to Kathy.

"Melissa dropped by yesterday and wanted to know when you'd be home," his mother said.

"I'll give her a call," Roy said, "and invite her out tomorrow night, perhaps see her this evening after we eat and catch up on the news."

"In fact, why don't we have her here for dinner here tonight? You two can go downtown after that."

Melissa worked as a data processing manager for her father's agribusiness firm, which included several local enterprises. She'd attended the local community college after high school, majored in business and computer science, and made predictable good progress with the family-owned company. Now twenty-two, she was at the peak of her attractiveness, Roy thought.

Helen had liked the girl since the two children were in high school. His mother was not one to push people together, he thought, although she'd like to see him married before too long. He'd made sure she knew that he did things at his own pace. She knew that rushing him would be fruitless, even counterproductive.

"Melissa? Hi, it's Roy. Just got back into town."

"Well, hi, stranger," she said. "You've been busy since the last time I saw you. You must tell me all about what *really* happened." Her silky voice had charmed him since they'd first met in high school. They'd dated on and off ever since. She'd come to his commissioning ceremony three years earlier.

"If you can come over for dinner tonight about six, I'll do that," he said. "Afterward, we'll go downtown."

"Or wherever," she purred. "I'd like that."

Later, Roy interrupted his conversation with his father to answer the door when it rang minutes before six.

"Hello, Roy," Melissa said in the voice that had always raised his blood pressure. Her blond hair glistened, brightened and outlined by the setting sun behind her. The dark blue dress set off her blue eyes and creamy skin. It appeared carefully selected for a dinner with the Hobbs family. Not the same one she'd pick for a carefree date with him.

She stepped in and clasped her arms around him. No one could see them from the living room. In seconds, they were locked in a kiss. The subtle smell of her perfume brought back memories of other evenings, other places. She hadn't changed that perfume in the years he'd known her. Perhaps because it worked, or because he'd once told her it was his favorite.

"I've really missed you," she whispered.

"Me, too, Melissa."

Her warm, sweet breath tickled his ear.

"You've been a busy fellow lately," she said. "The papers and TV have been full of what you did during that drug operation. And the engine room fire where you saved the man . . . how brave."

He took her hand as they walked back toward the kitchen. His mother had made a trip to the market and picked up fresh mushrooms, shrimp, and other things she knew Roy and the young woman liked. Cooking for Melissa was no mystery, Roy thought as he smelled the aromas that wafted across the room. Her favorites were as well known in this house as his own.

Over dinner, Melissa and the family made him retell all the details about the drug apprehension and how he'd come to be on the seized ship.

"The woman who was the prize crew skipper asked for me to be her engineer," he said.

"This is that Lieutenant Shannon we saw on CNN at the press conference in Miami?" his mother asked.

"Right."

"She's quite good-looking, Roy," his father said, looking up from his soup.

"She's as bright as she is attractive. Not to be trifled with when she has a gun in her hand, either." Better restrain his enthusiasm about Kathy with Melissa here, he thought.

"You mean she was shooting at those people herself?" Melissa said, her face a mask of disbelief.

"Of course. They were shooting at her, too. If I'd been on the bridge, I'd be firing back at them as much as anyone."

"I just can't imagine a woman being in a gunfight," Melissa said.

"Look at it this way," Roy replied. "Bullets are gender-neutral. You do what you have to do."

"Hmm," she said. "Tell us more about that fire in the engine room."

As he related the story, Melissa broke in.

"From what the papers said, that young man would have died if you hadn't gone into the smoke and pulled him out. You could have been overcome yourself."

"I had help. Other people were involved, too."

Roy would rather discuss what was new in Milledgeville, but that was not to be. He'd braced himself for repetitions of the story he'd already told a dozen times to various interviewers.

After dinner and polite socializing, Roy excused Melissa and himself. By then it was dark, too late to do more than take a walk on a cool, dry evening in a town where shops closed early.

"I must come to Mayport one weekend, have you tour me through that ship of yours," she said as they walked along.

"Good. There's plenty to see in Jacksonville."

They walked along the main street, greeted townspeople, and stopped several times to shake hands and chat. In between, they continued with small talk about neighbors and friends, who had new babies, who had moved away. Then, salted in among the harmless comments, was a stinger.

"What will you do, Roy," she said, "after you get out of the Navy?"

"I've decided to stay in," he said. "I like what I'm doing. Didn't know that when I started, of course, but it's a rewarding life."

"It won't always be exciting, you know, Roy," she said as she stopped and turned to face him. The cheerfulness had disappeared from her face.

"I know that. I couldn't stand this much excitement all the time." He took her hand and they walked on.

"You'll be away from home for six months at a time, live in strange, foreign places, and move around a lot. That will be tough on family life when you settle down. The whole idea sounds awful."

"I've thought of that. Look at it this way. Service life lets people see more of the world than staying in Milledgeville."

"What's wrong with Milledgeville? After what I hear about big cities, a small town is a better place to raise children these days."

"Nothing's wrong with the town. It's a fine place, full of good people, but there are other places to see, lots of other things to do."

"You have opportunities here. In no time, you'd make very good money, have a fine house. . . ."

"And live in that same fine house every day for the rest of my life, except for vacations and business trips? I used to dream of that, but being stuck in one place is not so attractive anymore."

"You've really changed since you went into the Navy, Roy." Her voice sounded harder now.

"No, but I understand what's out there in the big, wide world. Six months of traveling around the Mediterranean during a deployment taught me things I couldn't learn in school."

"Those sixteen-hour workdays at sea don't sound attractive."

"Other things make up for that. I had a real thrill when we captured those drug people and knew we stopped a big cargo of narcotics."

Melissa was silent for a moment as they walked along. "You'll never have the kind of life in the Navy that you could have here," she said. "Here you could earn a lot of money in a few years. You won't make anything working for the government."

"Money only matters as long as there's enough for a decent living. I don't want to be a millionaire. I'd rather be happy than rich."

"But you won't ever have any roots, any place to call home."

"If you have roots within yourself, know what you want, you can make a home anywhere."

"It's different for women," she said, her voice lower now.

For some women, he thought.

"How in the world did we ever start on this subject?" she asked as they walked back to his parents' house, where she'd left her new sports car. "Let's talk about something more pleasant." She put her arm around his waist as she used to when they were dating during college, as if to remind him of those times. The hug didn't feel as comfortable now, he thought.

At mid-morning the next day, Roy was repairing a light fixture for his mother when the phone rang. Melissa had recovered some of her good humor overnight.

"Mother and Daddy want to hear about your adventures, too. They'd like you to come for dinner tonight. If it's all right with you, we'll have our night out tomorrow."

"Sure thing," he replied.

The Elliotts had hired an excellent cook about five years earlier. Amanda Elliott, Melissa's mother, now kept busy with local charities, the library board, and other community activities.

When he arrived that night, wearing jacket, shirt, and tie, the Elliotts had trotted out the fine china and crystal. Or perhaps this was what they used all the time now.

When he was a boy, the Elliotts were building their business holdings in the area. Mrs. Elliott worked in the office, and cooked her own meals. Things had changed since then, as their big new antebellum-style house with a Jaguar and Cadillac in the driveway and Melissa's new sports car attested. There was money to be made in the county, and the Elliotts had cornered a goodly chunk of it, he thought.

After dinner, as the women prepared dessert, Milton Elliott took him aside.

"Like a cigar, Roy?" Elliott asked as he lifted the lid on a mahogany humidor.

"No thank you, sir, I don't use them."

"They're my only real vice," Melissa's father said. "Even with that, Amanda banishes me to the verandah to smoke them. Why don't we go out there while the ladies fix dessert?"

They sat in large padded rockers in the coolness of the Georgia evening on the porch. The aromatic smoke from Elliott's cigar wafted slowly away in the still air.

"You should be finishing up in the Navy some time soon. Wouldn't that be right, Roy?"

"Well, sir, I've decided to make the Navy a career."

"That's a mighty fine profession, Roy," Milton Elliott said as he rolled the expensive cigar in his hand. "The Navy, serving the country, is a noble calling. Just a shame that there's no money or future in it. About the time you'd be making your top dollar in a civilian job, you find yourself retired from the service, and have to start over again in the business world at middle age."

"I've considered all the pros and cons, sir," Roy said. "Service life has its hard spots, but it's still what I want to do with my life."

"Well, you know, Roy, things have changed a lot around here. My own business is a good example. It's hard to find self-starting managers with technical background, loyal folks who'll do a hard day's work. Your education and your experience in the Navy have taught you things that most young men don't know."

Melissa told him that I planned to stay in, Roy thought. That drove the dinner invitation, the prelude to this private man-to-man conversation. *Sounds like he's trying to make an offer I can't refuse.*

"I think that experience will come in handy for me in the future."

"I can make it come in handy for you *now*, Roy. I need someone to take the number-four job in my truck farming operation. Two of the managers in the jobs above you will retire within the next five years, just enough time to learn the business thoroughly. You know that I grow my management from within."

"That's very flattering, sir . . ."

"That job is only one example, Roy. We've been very fortunate here. You've grown up watching our business expand. We've succeeded by taking on the best people, and making them successful, too. We know you, know what you're made of. That's important."

"What you say is certainly worth serious thought, sir." No sense in turning the old boy down flat right now.

"Well, do think about it. Think about it hard. Not all the people you work for in places like the Navy are ones you get along with. You know the folks around here, and they know you, like you. That counts."

Mr. Elliott had never been to Europe, Roy thought, and would probably die without going there. Probably hadn't been west of the Mississippi more than a couple of times, either. His world was here in Milledgeville, and his way of doing things had brought him a fortune. By his standards, and those of most others in the town, Milton Elliott been a great success. Roy Hobbs, however, wasn't so sure.

The older man puffed on the cigar again.

"There's a lot to be gained in little towns like this, Roy. The city folks laugh at us, think we're hayseeds, but there's plenty of wealth and potential here."

"I'm not certain I'd want to spend my entire working life in Milledgeville, sir. I'd like to travel to Europe, other parts of the world. I've done some of that and I like it."

"A successful man who wanted to spend a few weeks in Europe each year could do that. There's also a good chance that our business will branch out," Elliott said, "and expand into foreign markets. The NAFTA treaty opens up opportunity and competition that we have to deal with. The European Union might provide other chances. That could involve a lot of foreign travel."

Elliott was upping the ante.

"That sounds exciting, sir."

"Well, I want to give you something to think about. The decisions you make now will affect the rest of your life. You should have the chance to make the right ones."

He used "decisions" in the plural. Did he also include Roy's future with Melissa as one of them?

A few minutes later, the door opened and Melissa appeared.

"I hope you two gentlemen have solved the world's problems, because dessert is ready," she said.

Thank heaven, Roy thought.

After dessert, Melissa said she wanted to take Roy out for a spin in her new sports car, on the interstate. Milton and Amanda Elliott seemed perfectly content about that.

The evening was cool in the small car with the top down. Instead of driving toward the interstate, Melissa turned the car down a country road that led to a place where they'd parked after dates years before. She turned onto a tiny side road, barely wide enough for the car, and pulled into a clearing where the full moon lit the place well enough to see the trees, and the fields beyond. Melissa shut the lights off and turned off the ignition. The silence of the night soon took over.

"How do you like it here?" she said.

"Just like the good old days."

"I remember," she said, and leaned toward him.

He'd kissed her here many times before. Then they'd talked for hours, about dreams and the future, about things they'd wanted to be, and do. Now neither of them was doing what they'd planned then. Her lips were close and inviting, and she expected to be kissed. He reached his hands over to the sides of her face and drew her closer.

When Melissa's kisses showed increasing fervor and length, the warmth in his face told Roy this was a good time for a break. Melissa wasn't quite so ready to stop.

"I enjoyed talking to your father tonight," he said.

She sat up straight.

"Did you two talk about ball scores, or business?"

"Business. He's trying to persuade me that the Navy's not the place for me, that Milledgeville is."

"He's right about that, Roy. Daddy's made a lot of money by being a smart old country boy, and plans to make a whole lot more."

"He said that. I reckon he will, too."

"I expect he offered you a job."

"The subject came up. He made life in Milledgeville sound very inviting, talked about long-term possibilities."

"He knows good talent . . . just as I do. There are better things than being alone on a ship for months at a time," she said as she ran her hand softly along his cheek and reached over to kiss him. "There are also advantages to having someone and someplace to come home to."

"True," he said, and pecked her cheek.

"So what did you tell him?"

"I told him I'd think seriously about what he said."

"And will you? Or is that a polite way to say no?"

"I'll consider what he said, which included things I didn't know before. That doesn't mean I'll change my mind, only that I'll take his offer seriously."

"He meant what he said. My father has high regard for you. He admires men who know what they're about. So do I."

"What will you tell your folks about how we spent the evening?" Roy asked.

"I'll tell them we parked out in a clearing all alone, of course . . . and let them imagine the worst."

"I doubt that. Then I could never come back to Milledgeville without worrying about finding your father with a shotgun."

"Well, surely, I wouldn't want that. I'll have to think up something else, something very innocent."

"Like the truth."

"Yes," she said, "like the truth."

"We'd better get back before their minds start to wander."

"We're big folks now," she said. "Whatever we do is not their business. It's between you and me. One of these days we ought to talk about that."

She started the car. The gravel crackled as she backed it around and headed slowly back through the narrow trail to the county road.

Yes, he thought, *one of these days real soon, we'll have to settle that.*

Chapter Twenty-one

The Hobbs house was dark when Roy returned at 11:40 P.M. He opened the door quietly; he knew his parents were long since asleep. They had never been ones to wait up for him.

He felt the warmth of Melissa's good-night kiss a moment ago, smelled the subtle, lingering scent of her perfume. The woman made a powerful argument to a man for coming home every night. Milledgeville, however, was no longer an option for him.

Roy sat in the darkened living room for a long time before he went up to bed.

Melissa had her comfort zone here, he thought. So did her father. The culture of the town made staying in Milledgeville natural for her, especially as one of the wealthy elite. Poorer folks across town yearned to get out, but couldn't. Those who could leave would stay, and those who'd leave were forced by economics to remain.

Why should Melissa become a junior officer's wife, live in government quarters in some foreign place where she was a nobody? Foreign to her meant any city more than a day's drive away. Why wait alone in Mayport, Norfolk, or San Diego for six months at a time while his ship was deployed to the Mediterranean or the Western Pacific? Her logical reaction was to maneuver him out of the Navy, and into her comfort zone.

Later, in bed, he stretched his arms out behind his head and reviewed the offers from both Elliotts. Melissa had persuaded her father to offer him a good job, Roy thought. The unspoken price, of course, would be to marry her. If Melissa wanted him, and he didn't want her, he'd have to look for a new job anyway.

Only two decisions a person makes in life matter, his father had said—the right occupation and the right person to marry. Even after one wrong decision, Dad reminded, you could be moderately happy. But heaven help those who decided both wrong. That rule, he thought, also applied to women now, including Kathy.

If a marriage to Melissa turned out poorly after he'd left the Navy to move back to Milledgeville, he'd be trapped. As he drifted off to sleep, Roy knew that his decision was now clear.

Upon awakening, Roy tried to frame what he'd say to Melissa, tried to find every way to soften the blow. They'd have dinner tonight, at her favorite restaurant outside town. The words couldn't be made easy. Thank heaven they weren't engaged. As distasteful as telling her would be, he must do that tonight.

His father had left for work when Roy came down for breakfast.

"You look like you've been out all night, Roy. Didn't you sleep well?" Helen asked.

"No, I sure didn't," he replied.

"Something happen last night?" she asked warily.

"Yes and no, Mom. This has been building up for a while. Might as well tell you about it."

His mother poured each of them a cup of coffee and sat down with him at the kitchen table.

"I should have seen this coming," he said, and curled up his fist.

"What are you talking about, Roy?"

"I'd told Melissa the night before that I planned to stay in the Navy," he answered. "That didn't please her at all."

"What do you mean?"

"I reckon she was banking on me to come back to Milledgeville, settle down, and propose marriage."

"Go on, Roy."

"Milton Elliott invited me outside after dinner, spent a half hour offering me good jobs if I'd get out and come back to Milledgeville. After I told him I planned to stay in, he tried to sweeten the pot with whatever it took to change my mind."

"And you haven't, of course."

'No. If anything, I'm more determined than ever."

"Good for you. Stick to your guns," Helen said. "You know why that conversation took place, don't you?"

"Of course. Not because I'm heroic and charming." Roy laughed. "Melissa must have told him what I said, and he decided that . . ."

"That he didn't want to lose the best son-in-law prospect in town," his mother continued. "And Melissa didn't want the best husband-candidate to get away, either. I can't blame them for that, but what matters is your happiness."

"They both want a piece of the action," he said, "and the action is me."

"You don't love her, do you, Roy?" His mother's voice had a tinge of sadness now.

He took a deep breath, let it out slowly.

"No, Mother, I don't. We've had a lot of fun together, but that's no reason to get married. She doesn't want to share my life, she wants me to accommodate to hers, and her father's. That would be fine if coming back here was what I wanted to do, but it isn't."

"Melissa's a nice girl, but if she's not the one who wants to share your dream, that's better to find out now than later."

"I don't want to hurt her, or let her believe there's hope when there isn't."

"Melissa wants a man who'll come home to a house in Milledgeville every night, where she can have her family nearby and continue to see friends she's known all her life."

"That's it," he said.

"I couldn't respect a husband who gave up his chosen profession for a secure job and the boss's daughter," Roy's mother said. "I don't understand how she could want a man on those terms."

"Mom, you've never spoken like this before."

"That's how I feel. No sense mincing words, especially about something this important."

"I especially don't want to hurt Melissa," he said.

"That's right, and it's what I'd expect of you. Why must you say anything to her?"

"You mean just let the relationship fade, wither on the vine?"

"Something like that. You've already told her that you intend to stay in the Navy, exactly what your feelings are. She's responded by having her father make you an attractive job offer. He also knows now how you feel. There should be no surprises."

Roy thought for a moment, and shook his head.

"That won't work with Melissa. I have to confront the truth, make a clean break once and for all."

"Roy, is there another girl?" his mother said.

"Why do you ask?"

"You said so many nice things about this Kathy Shannon since you came home. There's a gleam in your eye when you talk about her."

"I can't hide anything, can I?"

"Does she feel the same way about you?"

"I wish I could be sure. A young neurosurgeon from New York came to our award ceremony in Norfolk. I can only offer her what she already has. The question is what, and who, she wants."

"Does she know you're interested?"

"She knows, and she seems to like me. We spent a lot of time together in Key West after we brought the ship back. Kathy's in New York on leave now. I'm not sure I've moved fast enough, or how involved she is with the doctor. I'll talk to her when I return to the ship . . . if I'm not already too late."

"Kathy's a separate issue from Melissa, you know," his mother said. "You must deal with Melissa regardless."

"I know," he said.

"There are worse predicaments." Helen sighed. "If you can pick your problems, this is one of the better ones. You may not feel that way now, but believe me."

"There's not much time. I'll drive on back to the ship tomorrow." Roy stood up and sighed. "I'll settle this tonight with Melissa. Before that, I'd better replace the broken windshield-washer pump on your car."

When he'd returned from downtown with a new pump, his mother said Melissa had called. Her grandmother, now in her eighties, had suddenly been taken ill in Charlotte. Melissa had already left with her mother to go up there. There went his chance, he thought. Although he didn't look forward to his next meeting with her, he'd have to get on with it. Not a matter that could be handled on the telephone.

The following day, Roy arrived back at the ship after dark and parked the Chevy on the pier. The officer check-in board on the quarterdeck confirmed that Kathy had returned from leave. He'd see her tomorrow. They had to talk, he thought. He and Melissa had to talk, too.

Chapter Twenty-two

At 2300 the previous night, after a crowded flight from New York that arrived late, Kathy had stretched out on her bunk, tired but unable to sleep. The reading light by her head shone onto an open P. T. Deutermann novel, but she hadn't turned a page in the last twenty minutes. Only one whirlwind day of catch-up remained before the *Lockwood* returned to sea.

What she'd learned about Roy Hobbs since she returned to the ship tonight provided little solace. She'd overheard Gary Hartnett, the communicator, answer a question about Roy's whereabouts for another officer.

"Yeah, Paul, Roy's up home in Milledgeville courting his old flame," Hartnett had said. "I hear that Melissa's old man owns half the town, maybe half the county. Roy had a picture of her in his stateroom until recently. A good-looking woman. He'll come back to the ship smiling, I'll bet."

Kathy's face burned. She felt angry, used.

Her head throbbed. She'd gone down to sick bay after that, to get some aspirin from the duty corpsman. Bernadette Fiori stood with a clipboard in the small space, doing inventory on the medical supplies.

"Hi, Ms. Shannon," the tiny, dark-haired woman chirped. "How was leave in our old town? By the way, that Commendation Medal you recommended for me came in while you were away. Real nice of you to do that."

"Don't thank me—you earned it. New York was great, but right now I have a couple of boilermakers working inside my head."

"The chief's ashore, but I have just the thing," Fiori replied. "My own 'name brand' pain reliever, called Fiorinal."

"Are you pulling my leg?" Kathy asked warily.

"No, no, Ms. Shannon, that's what it's really called."

"I understand you straightened out QM1 Weatherby about harassment," Kathy said. "Good for you."

Fiori's demure appearance and soft-spoken voice made her look like anything but a fighting sailor. Maybe that fooled Weatherby.

"Susan clued me in after her problem," Fiori said. "The rest of us were ready for him."

When Kathy saw Roy Hobbs at breakfast the following morning, he smiled and raised his hand in greeting. She gave him a cool nod, then excused herself and walked out of the wardroom.

At mid-morning, she was working alone in the weapons office when Roy came in.

"Kathy, what did I do wrong?" he asked.

"Nothing," she answered, then turned away from him and back to her work.

"Come on, now. Something's eating you and I want to know what it is."

She remained silent.

"Kathy, answer me, please."

"Did you enjoy leave in Milledgeville?"

"That has nothing to do with why you're acting this way. Or does it?"

"You might ask Melissa."

"Ahh," he said.

She turned toward Roy and confronted him now.

"I don't go out with other women's boyfriends."

"Who said that Melissa is my girlfriend?"

"You drove up there to see her, didn't you?"

"I went to see my family, Kathy, what you presumably did in New York. Or did you spend your leave with Dana Mansfield?"

"Touché." She heaved a sigh. "I'm not seeing Dana anymore. That's over."

"I'm sorry and I'm not," he said. "I think you understand."

"No, I don't understand. I don't understand about you and Melissa, about what you were saying in Key West."

"And what were *you* saying in Key West, Kathy?"

"Dana and I dated periodically. Our relationship was never serious."

"Dana's eyes said differently in Norfolk. If that man wasn't in love with you, he was darn close. That was no sisterly kiss he strapped on you, either. Now what gives, Kathy?"

"I told you, Dana and I aren't seeing each other anymore." She'd almost snapped at him, she thought.

Hobbs took a deep breath. He seemed ready to ask another question, then hesitated.

"Does that mean you'll have dinner with me tonight, since neither of us have the duty and we sail tomorrow?" he said slowly.

"We haven't talked about you and Melissa."

"I went to high school with Melissa. We've dated off and on. That's it. In fact, I came close to telling her that we shouldn't see each other anymore."

"Why?" Kathy said.

"Melissa wants to get married; that's pretty clear. She

also wants a husband who'll come home at five o'clock every night. I'm not in love with her. I told her I was staying in the Navy, which is the truth.''

"That should give her a clear message."

"Not when her father offered me a high-paying job the following day. That sounds like upping the ante."

"You have to make up your mind, Roy," Kathy said, and turned back to her computer terminal.

"I did that about staying in the Navy months ago, and I also decided about Melissa. We want different things out of life."

"Did you tell her that?"

"She and her mother were called away by her grandmother's sudden illness. Otherwise, I would have told her the evening before I left."

"Seems like you could have told her before then, Roy."

"You weren't there at the time, Kathy," he snapped. "You don't know Melissa, or the situation, or her father, or the family relationships, or a whole lot of other things."

Roy was right, she thought. She had judged his actions based on what she might have done.

"Okay, I was wrong," Kathy said. "What you did is none of my business."

"Yes, it is your business, if you're also talking about us," he said.

"Us?" she said.

"Yes, us. I meant everything I said and did in Key West."

"Then you went back to Melissa on leave," she said.

"I went home to see my family on leave. What about you and Dana?"

"I told you we're not seeing each other anymore."

"Just like that. No explanation, no details."

"He told me during my leave that he loved me, wanted to marry me. I told him I was in the Navy for a career, that there's no way we could have a permanent relationship with his practice in one place and me in a hundred others."

"Do you love him, Kathy?"

"If we'd had any chance to be happy together, I could have loved him. We don't, never will. This is no one's fault. Nor is it the first time in history this has happened." She thought of telling Roy about Ken Lodge, but then thought better of it.

Roy came over and took her hand.

"Why don't we go and have that dinner tonight?" he said. "There's a neat place overlooking the St. John's River in Jacksonville. We can talk some more, perhaps come to understand things a little better."

Kathy hesitated for a moment.

"Okay," she looked down. "Okay, we'll do that."

"Let's leave around five-thirty. Then we can stroll along the riverfront afterward."

Kathy smiled and nodded. Roy leaned over and kissed her cheek before he turned away and closed the door gently behind him. *At least,* she thought, *I'm not too late.*

They drove along Atlantic Boulevard east to Mayport Road and turned north toward the Naval Station when they returned from dinner in Jacksonville. Roy parked his old car on the pier alongside the ship at 10 P.M.

The quarterdeck watchstander saluted as Kathy arrived at the top of the gangway.

"Evening, Ms. Shannon," the young petty officer said. "I have a nice surprise for you."

"Oh, what's that?"

He walked over to where watchstanders kept their logbook, then returned with a large bouquet of long-stemmed roses wrapped in cellophane.

"These came in for you about six o'clock," he said, smiling, and handed her the flowers.

"Why, thank you. Not every day the watch gets flowers delivered for someone."

"It's a first for me," he said. "Kinda nice idea, though. Enjoy, ma'am."

Roy watched while she opened the envelope clipped to the outside. *I love you. Please call me. Dana,* the message read. Kathy sighed and handed it to Roy.

He nodded, then handed it back without comment.

"Can I buy you a cup of coffee in the wardroom?" he asked.

"No, I'll pass for now." She stepped into the passageway leading to the interior of the ship and walked forward. The sound of machinery, blowers, and fans—the twenty-four-hour noise of a ship—filled her ears.

"Not the best place to kiss one's beloved good night," he said.

"We'll just have to make do, I guess." She looked up at him in the dim, red-lighted passageway.

"I hope those don't change anything," he said, nodding toward the flowers.

She hesitated for a moment, then sighed. "No. You know they don't. I wish he hadn't done that."

"But he did, and it's clear that he's hurting. I don't take any pleasure in that, you know."

"I know you don't, Roy. I'll call him tomorrow morning before we get under way."

"I don't envy you that."

"Thanks, I'll manage," she said.

"I love you, Kathy."

"I know. And I think I've come to realize that I love you, too, Roy."

He kissed her tenderly and touched her cheek. "Good night," he whispered.

"Good night, Roy."

Kathy turned and took the ladder leading below toward her stateroom, dreading the call she must make in the morning before they sailed.

Chapter Twenty-three

The steel deck of the USS *Lockwood* rose and fell beneath her feet as Kathy stood the forenoon watch as officer of the deck. A rolling ocean full of whitecaps from a tropical storm a hundred miles away made the ship pitch and shudder. Swells crashed in blue-green patterns over the bow. Her khaki shirt and trousers were damp from the spray, her hair tucked in a bun beneath a blue baseball cap. Her binoculars scanned what looked like an empty horizon.

She stepped inside and reached for the buzzing telephone behind her on the wall of the pilothouse.

"OD, Shannon," she said.

"Kathy, Mike Nelson in Combat Systems. Sonar reports a contact bearing 085, twenty thousand yards, moving south at five knots. We're designating him Sierra One."

Lieutenant (jg) Mike Nelson, the Combat Systems watch officer, sat amid consoles several decks below. He could detect everything within a hundred or more miles of the ship on radar and hear closer-in submarine contacts on sonar.

162

"What's your sonarman make of it, Mike? The first whale of the season, or a Russian transiting to Cuba?"

"Too early for the whale migration. Ivan could be running something into Cienfuegos. Not enough information yet. No radar return. That and the propeller noises say it's definitely not a surface ship. Recommend we go passive on sonar, deploy the SQR 19 towed array, and listen for his signature."

"Any U.S. or NATO subs reported transiting the area?" Kathy asked.

"Nothing on our printout down here," Nelson said.

"Thanks, Mike. Recheck that printout, please." She felt the back of her neck tingle.

She dialed the phone again and heard John Taylor's voice.

"Captain, Bridge. Sonar reports a submarine contact bearing 085, twenty thousand yards, designated Sierra One. No classification yet. Request permission to deploy the towed array and go passive."

"Make it so," Taylor said curtly, and hung up. Seconds later, the CO appeared on the bridge and slid silently into his chair. He tried to appear calm, but the scent of action had clearly captured his interest, Kathy thought. The skipper knew destroyers, but he was an unconvincing actor. She'd already given the order to stream the sonar array by wire behind the *Lockwood*, away from ship noises, to detect the sub's location and determine its characteristics.

Kathy's mind raced with possibilities. Despite *glasnost, perestroika*, and the demise of the Soviet Union, Russian submarines still operated off America's east coast. U.S. submarines, surface ships, P-3 Orion maritime patrol aircraft, and the SOSUS underwater sound network combined forces to keep track of them.

Five minutes later, the bridge phone buzzed again.

"Kathy, this is Mike. Sonarman Kyle is certain that the propeller noise is a Foxtrot."

Kathy knew Sonar Technician Third Class Eleanor Kyle.

The woman had an ear as sensitive as a tuning fork, an uncanny ability to distinguish subtle sounds, to filter out sea noises. The Russians had too many modern nuclear-powered boats to operate an old diesel Foxtrot this far from home, Kathy thought. She recalled they'd sold several such subs to third-world countries. Libya, India, Poland. Yes, and Cuba. Perhaps the Cuban Navy was shaking the rust out of one of their three. No way to be certain, or to query the sub for identity, she thought. Communications like the radio-telephone were not routinely available between surface and undersea vessels.

"Have Petty Officer Kyle run the tapes again, Mike. We have to be sure."

"She's already run them three times. The chief sonar tech listened to them, too. They agree the sub's signature has Foxtrot written all over it."

"Roger, thanks Mike."

"Captain, Sierra One is evaluated as a Foxtrot. Both Kyle and the chief sonarman are sure of it."

"Sound general quarters," Taylor ordered.

Kathy reached instantly for the switch on the after bulkhead. Muffled bell-like bongs rang throughout the ship. Even before the boatswains mate of the watch called the crew to general quarters seconds later, every sailor on the ship was running toward his or her battle station.

Throughout the frigate, watertight doors slammed shut, gun mounts and weapons systems swiveled, readiness reports poured in. Within five minutes, the United States Ship *Lockwood* was ready to go to war.

"Recommendation, OOD?" Taylor said.

The CO obviously knew what he intended to do. He wants to know if *I* have the right answers, Kathy thought.

"Report the contact up the chain by flash message, request the ready P-3 from NAS Jacksonville to drop sonobuoys, and run a MAD gear sector sweep, sir. Launch our LAMPS III helo to deploy dipping sonar. Ready the

MK50 ASW torpedoes. We can be ready to work a coordinated ASW problem before the P-3 arrives on station.''

"Make it so." The CO nodded.

Kathy turned to her junior officer of the deck a few feet away and saw him quickly writing the message draft. She lifted the phone to order the launch of the ship's SH-60 Seahawk helicopter.

"What if he turns toward us, Shannon?" the captain asked.

"Recommend we fire only if we hear him open outer torpedo tube doors," she said. "He may not be looking for trouble." That, she knew, was a submarine's last preparation before firing an anti-ship torpedo. Uncomfortable dampness soaked her underarms.

"... and if he launches his torpedoes before we fire ours?" the captain said . . . "We could all be dead for waiting that long." His eyes were riveted on her now.

"He's too far out for that now, sir. No current intelligence supports an imminent attack by anyone. If we fire before he opens doors, we've initiated an aggressive act, indefensible at a court of inquiry. If he opens doors, we have clear hostile intent."

For the first time she could remember in recent weeks, John Taylor smiled.

Fifteen minutes later, *Lockwood*'s air search radar picked up the P3C Orion antisubmarine aircraft barreling toward their location. The radio speaker crackled as the P-3 pilot established communications with the ship.

Windblown lookouts with binoculars pressed to their eyes scoured the horizon for signs of a periscope amid whitecapped seas. A few minutes later, the gray-and-white turboprop aircraft, a long, tapered magnetic detection device stretched outward from its tail, began a graceful circular sweep of the area.

"Uh-huh, I do believe you have a submarine down there," the P-3 pilot's voice said over the speaker.

"Where is the sub now?" Taylor barked.

"Bearing 095, range fifteen thousand yards," Kathy said. "He hasn't changed course or speed since acquisition. He surely knows we're here, sir."

"Yes," Taylor replied, "he's probably picked us up on the passive side of his high-frequency sonar. Hasn't gone active, hasn't changed anything. Is he trying to tell us he's making a peaceful transit, or waiting to lull us until he swings around and lets fly?"

"He'll know our ship class from our propeller sounds," Kathy said, "and what ASW systems we carry. When the P-3 drops sonobuoys, he'll know they're up here. That would make a run on us suicidal. He'd also have to close in to attack. I don't think Fidel wants his submarines to tangle with us."

"What if you're wrong, Shannon? What if he's a rogue Libyan out there, or someone else with an axe to grind?"

"We'll have more than enough time to react if he changes course toward us. I say he won't. If he starts a run on us, we have enough ordnance to spoil his afternoon. If I'm right, sir, we won't have to start a war."

Taylor smiled again.

The radio barked out a scratchy exchange between the P-3 pilot and the combat systems watch below decks, isolating the last known location, or datum, of the sub.

Kathy watched through binoculars as a pattern of radio-equipped sonobuoys fluttered down from the P-3 and splashed into the water where *Lockwood*'s sonar had estimated the sub to be. The miniature sonars would both locate the sub and let him know they were there, she thought.

The voice of the P-3 pilot crackled over the tactical radio net a few minutes later. "Sierra One is not changing course, depth, or speed, no evasive maneuvers," he said.

"Roger," Kathy acknowledged. The ship's LAMPS III helicopter hovered near the last known location of the sub. A dipping sonar at the end of a long wire pulsed to confirm the submarine's location. Must be getting pretty tense down below for that sub skipper.

Minutes later, the bridge phone rang again.

"Bridge, Combat Systems. Kathy, the Foxtrot has dropped off our sonar picture. We guess he's dived for the thermocline to shake us in the cold water," Nelson said.

The tingle on the back of Kathy's neck returned. *Or he's diving for cover ready to launch a torpedo if we close him,* she thought.

She reported the lost contact to the skipper. His brows knitted.

"What do you recommend now?" Taylor said slowly.

"Expanding search pattern starting at the datum, keep the P-3 on station, work the problem until we're sure of the Foxtrot's intentions. He may still be trying to evade, but we have to be ready for an attack in case he isn't."

For three tense hours, they searched the ocean like a hound sniffing after a rabbit. The ship and the P-3 covered hundreds of square miles of ocean with sonar signals and detection sweeps. Then the phone buzzed again on the bridge bulkhead.

"Bridge, Combat Systems. We've got him back, Kathy! Kyle says its definitely the Foxtrot again."

"What's he doing?"

"His heading will take him directly into Cienfuegos." Aside from initially trying to evade them, the Foxtrot had not changed course, she thought. *He knows we're here and is ignoring us.*

"What do you think now, Lieutenant Shannon?"

"I say he wants to go home to Mom and the kids. If he wanted to tangle, he'd have continued to evade and then come back. He just wants to be left alone."

"Send a message saying that unless otherwise directed, we are breaking off contact," Taylor said, "that the Foxtrot appears headed for Cuban waters. Secure from general quarters." The CO climbed out of his chair and walked back toward his sea cabin.

"Aye, aye, sir." She glanced at the JOOD, who again took his message pad in hand. Boats Johnson looked at her.

She nodded, and he stepped to the 1MC announcing system. ''Now secure from general quarters. Set the regular under way steaming watch. On deck Section Three,'' he said.

Taylor purposely kept her on the bridge to prosecute the contact, Kathy thought. Perhaps he wanted to sound out her tactical savvy. He hadn't seen her perform during the drug confrontation. His smile at her performance today had been a first.

Chapter Twenty-four

Wardroom dinner conversation that evening had become an informal ''hot wash-up'' of the Foxtrot incident, Kathy thought. The CO ate his dessert and drank coffee silently as the younger officers reviewed the afternoon's operations.

''Kathy, why didn't you move in when we picked him up again, ping him with active sonar, let him know we were breathing down his neck?'' the operations officer said.

''The P-3's sonobuoys and the dipping sonar from our LAMPS III helo told him what we had out here,'' Kathy replied.

The ops boss, a newly promoted lieutenant, shook his head. ''You should have prosecuted the contact more aggressively, let him know we mean business.''

''In international waters? In peacetime, with no intelligence warning, zero aggressive reaction by the submarine? We're not here to start a war. That boat's captain will tell his superiors they can't operate around here without the Americans engaging.''

Some heads nodded; a few looked toward the CO.

''You should have acted more boldly with him,'' the ops

boss said. "Submariners only understand it when you let them know you've got them cold."

"If this were wartime, I would have jumped and finished that Foxtrot before he could load his torpedo tubes," she said softly. She paused for only a second. "I'd have treated him like a boatload of drug traffickers."

No one spoke.

John Taylor broke the silence. "Lieutenant (jg) Shannon called it right. She recommended an ASW torpedo release if the sub opened outer doors. There's a careful line between protecting your own ship and creating an international incident which the President must answer for."

He leaned forward in his chair. His eyes looked around the table, scanning each officer in turn.

"The Foxtrot made exquisitely clear he wasn't looking for trouble," Taylor said. "If he'd been a surface ship, even a Cuban patrol boat, we would have exchanged flashing light messages or bridge-to-bridge radio and gone on our way. We don't play cat and mouse simply because it's a submarine. Remember that for the future, gentlemen. Good job today, Kathy. Bravo Zulu." The skipper rose and walked out the wardroom door into the after passageway.

The Navy shorthand for "well done" was the first time John Taylor had praised her in front of her peers, or called her by her first name. When she looked over at Roy, he was grinning. She smiled back, then headed for the weapons office to finish up paperwork before turning in. She had the 0400–0800 morning watch and needed sleep after a stressful day that had begun at 0600.

A minute after she settled down to work in the weapons office, the door opened and Roy entered.

"Could hardly believe my ears down there," he said. "Maybe you've made a believer out of him, Kathy."

"Surprised me, too, but that's only one time," she said, rising from her chair to face him. "You remember the old Navy rule about one foul-up erasing a hundred 'attaboys.' "

"Come closer," he said. "I want to give you another 'attaboy.' I missed you." He raised her chin slightly with his finger and kissed her.

Her arms curled around him; her lips found his again.

"Me, too," she replied. The hug, the closeness of him, felt good. There hadn't been enough of this lately.

"How did your conversation with Dana work out the other morning?"

"Reached his answering machine when I called at 0630 from the pier before we got under way. He'd probably been called into the hospital on a surgical emergency. I left word about us." She suppressed the fleeting thought that he might have been at another woman's place.

"Maybe he'll understand now," Roy said. "I know you're being kind to him. Your kindness is one of the things that makes me love you."

He hugged her.

"Some people might find that hard to understand after the drug boat ramming," she said.

"I don't. You didn't want any of those people to be killed. You didn't start the fight. Kathy Shannon had a job to do, and she did it . . . and I love her."

He kissed her once, then again, then a third time. She wished they were someplace else, somewhere where they could be alone.

"We need to talk about the future, too," he said.

She nodded. "I know."

"My sea-duty tour will be up here six months before yours, as I reckon it. They'll either transfer me to another ship, or ashore for a school or shore duty. I'm going to put in a six-month extension request to make our tour lengths come out even."

Kathy hadn't focused on that yet.

"We'll soon be common knowledge around the ship," he said, "such as when we spend time together like this, or go ashore together."

"I thought about what that might mean to the other

women," Kathy replied, "whether it's an encouragement to something we don't want to foster . . ."

"We have a right to live, too. As long as we keep what we do honest and above board, no one has any reason to complain," he said.

"Like not coming to my stateroom, even on business?" she said.

"Right," he said.

"I'll call my father when we make port. Chances are Dana has already told him."

"Your daddy will have every reason to be disappointed that you chose the Georgia cracker over the promising young surgeon," Roy said, smiling, "but it's not his opinion I'm concerned with."

"Don't worry about that. My sister didn't marry the doctor he tried to fix her up with either, and everything's worked out fine for her. Perhaps Dad will learn after a while."

Jeff Levine met her on deck a couple of days later. "Roy Hobbs came in this morning with a six-month extension. I told him I'd recommend it. That makes his rotation date the same as yours. Any coincidence there?"

"Yes, XO. Roy and I are seeing each other."

"Must be serious if he's ready to extend."

"It is, but we're not advertising that."

"That's your business, and I'll respect your privacy, but it's hard to keep secrets aboard ship." Levine smiled.

"I guess I'm about to find out how hard, sir."

"Well, good luck to both of you. The old man probably wouldn't encourage this, you know."

"The skipper has nothing to worry about. I can imagine his concerns."

Levine nodded.

"Have you set a date?"

"Not yet. We have a year and a half before transfer, unless something off the wall happens."

"Like your being shanghaied to CINCLANTFLT's personal staff?"

"How did you know about that?"

"The EA up there is an old skipper of mine. We spoke on the phone after the awards ceremony."

"Does the skipper know?"

"I figured if you wanted him to know, you'd tell him."

"Right, XO, and I haven't."

During the sea detail tie-up when they returned to Mayport a few days later, Kathy noticed a well-dressed blond woman on the pier next to a shiny red sports car. Few wives came down when the ship returned from short operations, and she didn't look like any Kathy knew. Most worked; the others stayed home with children. She thought little of it and went back aft to finish up other business.

Kathy looked up when she heard the word passed for Lieutenant (jg) Hobbs to call the quarterdeck. Minutes later, she saw the blond woman, who now stood on the quarterdeck, put her arms around Roy and kiss him warmly. That had to be Melissa.

From Kathy's vantage point on the 01 level above them, they seemed to have an animated conversation. Surely, Roy had not invited her down for the weekend, and then neglected to uninvite her after their conversation and before the ship sailed. A few minutes later, the blond left the ship, climbed into the red sports car, and roared quickly off the pier. Kathy climbed down from the 01 level before Roy entered the after passageway. He saw her and came over.

"Melissa," he said, his face red. "She invited herself for the weekend. I told her once that she should come down and see the ship and all that, but it was a polite, generic invitation. Sorry, Kathy, it's unlike her to do something like this."

"Oh?" Kathy said.

"Kathy, I'm sorry. I had no idea, but now that she's here, I'll settle things once and for all."

"You have lipstick on your cheek," she said.

Roy blushed, snatched the handkerchief from his back pocket, and scrubbed away at the red spot.

"I'm taking Melissa to lunch today in Jax. I'll settle things then."

"There must be more to her impromptu appearance than a simple visit," Kathy said.

"Melissa said she'd been selfish to insist that I get out of the Navy and come back to Milledgeville. She claimed she was ready to go wherever I went."

"What do you think about that, Roy?"

"I love *you*. That's what I think. Nothing else matters. Too bad I wasn't able to settle this with her before I came back down here."

"Roy, any man with two women in love with him has a problem," Kathy said.

"I don't love her, Kathy. I also told you I didn't want to hurt her, but she's left me no alternative."

"Stand by. She'll probably slap your face and stomp out saying that she'll hate you forever."

"I'll take care of it," he said, then exhaled heavily. "I'm leaving about eleven. See you after lunch, if you still plan to be on the ship after liberty goes down."

"I'll be here," she said. "Good luck."

He started bending toward her to kiss her, then must have realized where they were and straightened up.

"Thanks, Kathy. I do love you."

"I love you too," she replied. "Don't forget that."

"Melissa," he said, "there's no way. I'm not in love with you. You wouldn't be happy with me and traveling around the world like a gypsy. You've said as much. I'm sorry. I'm not trying to hurt you."

They'd been talking about his change of heart. Roy had been angling for the right time, the least hurtful way to say the obvious. He knew now that he had never loved her. Fun was one thing, but love was different.

"There's another woman, isn't there?" Melissa said. "There's been one all the time, hasn't there? I knew there was something wrong when you came up home. Why couldn't you just be honest with me?"

"Yes," he said. "Her name is Kathy Shannon. She's an officer on the ship. And yes, I am in love with her."

"You're a two-timing snake, Roy Hobbs, and I'm *glad* I will never have any more to do with you!" Melissa said, her eyes red, handkerchief to her nose. "You've strung me along for months, years . . . all these women behind my back. Your name will be mud in Milledgeville." She sobbed. "They'll know you for the lying, cheating, sad excuse for a man you are. I'll tell them the *real* story behind their big naval hero."

"Now wait just a minute, Melissa," Roy said. Where did she get "all these women"?

She ignored him.

"You better *not* decide to get out of the Navy, because there'll never be a job for you within a hundred miles of Milledgeville. I'll see to that. You better stay with your wonderful Navy and your seagoing girlfriend. I hope she learns what a miserable conniver you are and gives you a dose of your own medicine."

Melissa pulled a compact from her purse, flipped it open, and looked in the mirror. She wiped streaked mascara off with a tissue, threw everything back in her handbag, and suddenly stood up.

"Now you'll have to excuse me. I have some important things to tend to at home."

So much for breaking it to her gently, Roy thought as Melissa stormed out of the fashionable Jacksonville restaurant without looking back. When the waiter came over, he ordered another beer and said that the lady would not be returning. The waiter nodded. She'd made enough of a scene, Roy thought, that the reason must be clear. He felt suddenly tired, although it was only twelve forty-five. At the same time, he was relieved.

Roy took a long sip of the fresh draft beer and thought of the discussion Melissa had just concluded. Whoever said "hell hath no fury like a woman scorned," sure had it right.

He paid the bill and walked for a few blocks in the cool afternoon sunshine to gather his thoughts. By evening, Melissa would be back in Milledgeville. By this time next week, his reputation there would, indeed, be mud, except among those who knew him well, and others with a healthy distrust for the Elliotts. If Melissa went through with what she'd said, she'd cause herself as much damage as she'd ever do him. That was her problem, he thought.

When he returned to the car, Roy paused for a moment. Things could be worse, he told himself. He could be married to Melissa. There was more to be grateful for than he'd expected. Roy spotted a local pay phone and decided to call his mother.

"That's too bad, son," Helen said, "but we learn a lot about people from situations like this, don't we?"

You surely got that one right, Mama.

Roy arrived back aboard *Lockwood* just before 2:00 P.M. The CO had declared liberty for three-quarters of the crew, and launched everyone but the duty section on an extended weekend with families and loved ones. He walked up to the weapons office to look for Kathy.

She looked up when he came in the door, and smiled. She stood up and went and put her arms around him.

"Bad?" she asked.

"Like a root canal without novocaine," he muttered.

"Not graceful about it, was she?"

"How did you know?"

"You look like you've been kicked in the stomach, for one thing," Kathy replied.

"Makes me wonder why I worried so much about hurting her."

"It's over," Kathy said. "You can be grateful for that."

"Yes, it's over . . . for sure. The good news is I learned

that I'm in love with the right woman," he said, and drew her to him after he reached back to close the door. He kissed her again and again until her knees felt weak and her cheeks burned, until she tried halfheartedly to pull away from him, failing because she didn't want to succeed.

"Let's get off this ship," he said, "and go into Jacksonville and find some fun. We can drive over one of those bridges I haven't burned yet."

Chapter Twenty-five

The following evening, Kathy met Roy in the weapons office after dinner. The few kisses and hugs these meetings yielded were never enough, but all that shipboard life would allow.

A few minutes later, after Roy had left to handle eight o'clock reports as engineering department duty officer, she turned to pick up her Naval Academy class ring. She'd taken it off while working at the computer because her fingers had swollen. It was gone. *Should have put the darn thing in my pocket.*

Kathy treasured the gold ring, the symbol of four years of hard work at Annapolis. For a half hour, she scoured the office, then went below and searched her stateroom. Could she have taken it off absentmindedly and left it somewhere else? Not very darn likely.

No chance it had been stolen, she thought. The only one who'd been around was Roy. Well, it didn't walk away. The ring had little value to anyone else, except that it was solid fourteen-karat gold with a large inlaid amethyst. The following day Kathy asked the department yeoman, Seaman Tom Walsh, to keep an eye out for it.

Two evenings later, when Kathy had the weapons department duty, she and Roy met in the office, as usual, after dinner. She had taken to remaining aboard to be with him on nights when he had the duty, and he had done the same.

They never locked the office door, for no one ever came up to work after dinner while in port. Both crew and officers watched a recent movie on the ship's internal television system, so few people walked around the ship after dinner. Besides, she thought, unlocking the door if someone knocked would create greater speculation about what had been going on.

Roy had just taken her into his arms and was kissing her, when suddenly the door swung wide open. Seaman Walsh looked in, muttered "Oops," and hastily closed the door.

"The cat's out of the bag now," Roy said.

"Do you think Walsh will say anything? He's a pretty sensible type," Kathy responded.

"Two officers in an embrace aboard ship would be too juicy a bit of scuttlebutt for any sailor to resist. Now wouldn't the word get around if, for example, someone saw Walsh kissing Sonar Tech Eleanor Kyle up here?"

"Well, I . . ."

"Men are just as gossipy as women, worse if anything," Roy said. "This was only a matter of time. Could have been worse, I suppose."

"No it couldn't. We've never done nothing to be ashamed of," Kathy said, "and we're not breaking any regulations. It's just that the system discourages shipboard romances. I'm simply not going to worry about it."

"We better get accustomed to doing without privacy around here."

"What if we announce to everyone that we're going together?" she asked.

"Might be a real good idea. Let me think about that.

Meanwhile, I'll head down to the wardroom for the movie,'' he said, and reached over to kiss her again.

"I'll join you in a few minutes,'' she said. "I'm going to take another look for that class ring.''

While on her knees searching, Kathy heard a tap on the door. She chuckled to herself. That had to be Walsh again, knocking to be sure this time.

"Come in,'' she said, looking up to see that she was right. The young sailor, one of Sam Apriliou's men who'd been with her on the initial boarding party to the *Marialena*, looked nonplused. "I'm still looking for my missing class ring,'' she said.

"Sorry about barging in on you before, Ms. Shannon. I didn't think anyone was here. I should have knocked.''

"That's all right,'' she said. "I would have done the same thing.'' Kathy shrugged.

"I'll keep that to myself, Ms. Shannon. It's no one else's business.''

"Thank you. You're very thoughtful to say that,'' she replied. She'd always had a good rapport with Walsh, as she had with most people on the ship. Perhaps he was trying to do the right thing.

"I came up to get my gunners mate 3rd blue book,'' he said, squeezing past her to reach into the bookcase above the file cabinets in the tiny office. He pulled out a training manual.

Walsh smiled and drew the door closed more slowly behind him as he left.

She walked down to the wardroom a few minutes later and joined three duty section officers watching a TV movie. How nice it would be to hold Roy's hand at times like this, cuddle up next to him on the wardroom sofa, but that would never happen. Nor could Roy ever be seen exiting her stateroom, or she leaving his, especially now. Being surprised in the office, as innocent as that was, could still haunt them.

Why was it so all-fired important to keep up false appearances, not show any emotion toward someone you loved? Then she thought of most people on the ship, whose love interests remained ashore. It was unfair to remind them.

Kathy and Roy walked on deck for fresh air after the movie. Strong floodlights bathed the pier in light, creating dark shadows in most of the areas on the ship. Tonight's events had changed things.

"We have a lot to think about," Roy said. "Perhaps Seaman Walsh did us a favor."

"You're right," she said. "I have some other things to ponder. The future's more complicated for me than it is for you."

"Let's talk about any problems. Your future plus mine equals ours."

"I know," she said. They talked for a while, stole a few kisses, then went separate ways to their staterooms.

Kathy sat on her bunk in the darkness of her small cabin. Marriage and kids would not be as simple as it had been for her sister, Fiona.

Separation would be inevitable sooner or later. The only way to avoid it, she thought, would be never to love anyone. That wouldn't work. She had someone to love, and having him around part of the time was better than having no one around all of the time, or at least no one who mattered. Life meant more than a succession of affairs, a series of charming, handsome men who would parade through her life. Not her style, Kathy thought.

Then, children. The kids were Fiona's treasure, and Kathy loved the two of them. She hadn't thought much about children until Roy came along. What was it about love that maked you want to have a man's children? she wondered. Something to bring the relationship to its fullness.

Kathy read for a while, then turned in. Was commanding a warship what she most wanted in life, or were other, more basic things more important?

Her father had been right. You couldn't have it all your own way. Everyone must make choices, decisions, promises from which they couldn't uncommit themselves. She was ready to do this with Roy, she thought. They'd become closer in a few weeks than most people did in years. Sharing life-threatening experiences had stripped away pretensions about each other.

Make up your mind. You haven't walked away from anything yet, or have you? Were you right to reject Ken Lodge and Dana? Yes, she thought, *but I'd be wrong to walk away from Roy.* Besides, she didn't want to. She wanted to be closer to him, to hug him night after night, to be with him where they could be truly alone, and fully together.

She had never wanted a man like this before. The urgency of his kisses lately told her it was the same with him. What was wrong with that? What could be more natural, more expected, with the person you love? As drowsiness finally washed over her, Kathy Shannon knew it was time to make some important decisions, and stick by them.

The next morning, Roy came up to her on deck about ten-thirty where she was talking to Boats Johnson. Roy waited until they finished, then took her aside. "I've figured out a way," he said, "to solve this problem of our relationship and the word getting around to the crew."

"Sounds as though you stayed up all night thinking about it," she said lightly.

"No, but I did give it a lot of thought after our visit by Seaman Walsh."

"I did some hard thinking last night, too," she said.

"Part of mine," he said, "was to wish that we had spent last night together, in each other's arms. Does that shock you?"

"No, probably because I would have liked the same thing."

"Okay, that settles it," he said. "You come with me." He took her hand firmly in his, something he'd never done aboard ship before, led her quickly down the port side of the ship toward the quarterdeck, past men of her division working outside on the guns and the decks. His legs were longer, his strides broader than hers. She struggled to keep up with him. Roy climbed down the forward ladder from the bridge to the main deck with her behind him. He continued aft through the port passageway. They were now near the quarterdeck. He took her hand again and walked over to the brow where the junior officer of the deck stood.

"Permission to leave the ship, sir," he said. He climbed to the top of the ladder and saluted the OOD and the colors aft. Kathy did the same and followed him to the bottom of the brow. Halfway down, he reached back and took her hand. She felt the eyes of the crew on them, and knew everyone was wondering what these two officers were doing.

When he reached the bottom of the brow, he turned to her.

"Now, Lieutenant," he said, drawing her close to him. "I'm going to give you three things. The first one is easy. You're going to have to think about the other two."

"Roy Hobbs, what are you talking about?" Kathy wriggled, trying without success to get out of his grasp. "Why are you holding me like this in front of all these people. Everyone on the ship is looking at us!"

"Good. Then there can't be any more questions or speculation about us anymore, can there? No more doubt in anyone's mind?"

"Well . . ."

"I just want to make sure there's none on your part," he said. His normally soft eyes were determined, piercing now.

"Why, no, why should there be?" she said.

"Good. Here's the first thing I want to give you."

Kathy expected a kiss, but instead, Roy reached into his pocket and pulled out her Naval Academy class ring.

"Roy, where did you *ever* find that?"

"I didn't. I borrowed it."

"Borrowed it? Why the devil did you do that?" she

scolded. "Don't you know I've been looking all over the ship for that ring for days? You mean you've had it all the time, and let me search and search . . ." She started to pull away from him, but he wouldn't let her.

Kathy glanced toward the ship. The entire deck watch and the men on the upper deck had stopped work. Some leaned on brooms and swabs, others hung over railings. All were looking at their division officer being held close by that engineer, Lieutenant Hobbs.

"Sorry, Kathy, but I think you'll understand. . . ."

"You better have a pretty good story. . . ."

"This might be good enough," he said as he pulled a small, velvet-covered dark-blue box from his pocket and flipped up the top. A pear-shaped blue-white diamond of about one carat in a white gold setting stared up at her.

"I didn't know any other way to get your ring size."

"Roy . . ." Suddenly she was lost for words. Suddenly, she didn't care about the troops on the ship watching them, what people would say, even if the captain lectured them.

"The right answer is 'yes,' " Roy said. "Now, would you like to hear the question?"

"Yes . . . I mean, no, I mean it's all right, you don't have to . . ."

"Lieutenant, you're going to have to make up your mind," he said, smiling now. "About this, and when you'd like to have that honeymoon in Key West."

"I've made up my mind and the answer is yes," she said.

"That leaves only one unfinished piece of business, then." He slid his arms around her and kissed her, holding her close as he lifted her off the ground. As Kathy lost herself in this very public kiss in the middle of the day, she heard cheering, whistles, and clapping. She looked toward the ship where the men of her division stood. Those not clapping and cheering were holding their thumbs up and smiling.

"I do believe we've given everyone something to talk about over lunch today," he whispered to her.

As she and Roy walked back aboard ship, the bright diamond now on her left hand, she saluted the colors and the OOD. The young messenger of the watch who had handed her the flowers from Dana was smiling.

"Gee, Ms. Shannon," the sailor said, "I sure hope this doesn't mean the whole squadron's going to start calling us the *Love Boat*."

Kathy and Roy laughed. Somehow, they knew they were home.

Epilogue

Lieutenants (jg) Kathleen Ann Shannon and Roy Hobbs, USN were married in the U.S. Naval Academy Chapel at Annapolis, Maryland, the following June. Lieutenant Commander Jeff Levine, Executive Officer of USS *Lockwood*, was best man. Kathy and Roy honeymooned in Key West, spent several evenings reliving the magic of Mallory Dock and Duval Street.

Both were later selected early for promotion to Lieutenant based upon their personal decorations for valor and performance. USS *Lockwood* received a Meritorious Unit Commendation from the Commander-in-Chief of the U.S. Atlantic Fleet. Commander John Taylor was assigned ashore at the end of his command tour to a job in the Plans and Policy Division of the Office of the Chief of Naval Operations. His new boss is Rear Admiral Allison Douglas O'Hara, a naval aviator.